ASHEN HEART

ASHEN HEART

THE BLOOD BOUND SERIES, BOOK II

SABRINA VOERMAN

ASHEN HEART: THE BLOOD BOUND SERIES, BOOK TWO
BY SABRINA VOERMAN
PUBLISHED BY QUILL & CROW PUBLISHING HOUSE

Cover Design by Fay Lane

Interior by Cassandra L. Thompson

Printed in the United States of America

ISBN (ebook) 978-1-958228-47-0

ISBN (print) 978-1-958228-48-7

Library of Congress Control Number: 2024904510

Publisher's Website: quillandcrowpublishinghouse.com

For T.R. Tells,
You taught me that embracing the darker side of my characters was okay.

THE BLOOD BOUND SERIES

BY SABRINA VOERMAN

Weaving the real world with fantasy, The Blood Bound Series features four books inspired by history and brimming with magic. Witches, werewolves, vampires, and sirens are at the helm of the series, featuring an overarching story that expands over centuries.

Packed with feminist themes and macabre storytelling, small connections between the first three books tie them together for the final book. The series features three books that stand alone and can be read in any order, each laying the groundwork for the finale.

A NOTE FROM THE PUBLISHER

Please consult the back of the book for content warnings. Index A is a helpful guide to understand the Blood Bound Series timeline. Index B includes a list of potential triggers.

PROLOGUE
THE YEAR OF THE PINES

Eighty Years Before the Coven

Fires, from within its humble homes, made the town of Silvania look charming from a distance. Trees toughened by years of harsh weather surrounded it. They stood naked, great heaps of snow sloughing off their branches when it grew too heavy. Thunderous crackling sounded when the weaker branches finally gave way, breaking under the pressure before landing in the thick snow with subtle grace.

The glow of the fire extended from the hearth, warming the sisters. Torenia sat with her shoulders back, her dress splayed around her, hands firmly clasped in her lap. Aster, her younger sister, squirmed, unable to sit still and listen to the story Mama was reading them.

The dusty book was tattered, its spine broken in various spots, the leather binding exposing its insides like a body sliced open, bones and organs spilling out. Torenia held her breath, afraid her exhalation might blow the book apart and she'd never hear another story again. What a horrible life it would be to have no stories before bed.

The December chill crept in through the windows, fogging them and leaving sparkling frost around the edges of the glass. Torenia tucked her elbows into her sides, keeping her hands clasped to show Mama what a proper young girl she was, to prove that she was a good daughter. Still, Mama smiled warmly at Aster, barely glancing at Torenia.

Mama held the book and studied the words in front of her with dark brown eyes, weighing them before she spoke. Finally, her velvet voice filled the room. "In the bitter cold winter, during the Year of the Curse, a wicked witch was approached by a pretty young woman. The witch did not trust her, so she set a curse upon the woman's husband. The woman was an adulteress—the worst kind of woman—and the witch used him to murder her. The man turned into a wicked beast, a creature that lurked in the darkness of night, preying upon the young ladies of the town who had deviated from the path of righteousness."

She turned the page, studying her daughters with a raised eyebrow. Her eyes hardened when she landed on Torenia before she looked back at the book—suspense built within her bated breath. The crinkled old page flipped before she continued.

"The wicked witch controlled the man-wolf, turning him loose upon those who wronged her. But the witch was caught for her evil-doing and was burned at the stake in the very woods where she practiced her Craft. Some say she did not deserve it, but remember, girls, witchcraft and adultery are *both* a crime." She paused to look at her daughters, both of whom were too young to know what adultery meant, though they hung on her every word. "Despite her treachery and undeterred by death, the witch also cursed the beast with the inability to die. So, as the years went by, her descendants learned to control the beast, turning him loose upon anyone who dared question their authority or their right to power. Some say he still haunts these woods today, for he is bound to the witch's descendants or whoever holds the scroll to summon him."

"Mama, are we the wicked witch's des... desce..." Aster struggled to pronounce the word, unfamiliar to her five-year-old tongue.

"Some believe we are," Mama replied before closing the book.

Torenia wished the story wouldn't end, for she longed to hear the rest, every last detail about witchcraft. Instead, thanks to Aster's big mouth, Mama had a warning for them. "We do not speak of it, for your father is the mayor, and a stain on his name is a stain on us all. Above all, we must help your father continue his path to greatness. Should there be any whisper of witchcraft on the lips of our neighbors, it would be the end of us. Promise me, girls, you will never even speak the word 'witchcraft' outside of our home. Promise me you will never participate in such atrocities and shed light on all those who practice."

"We promise," they both mumbled, Torenia somewhat more enthusiastically. But Mama's eyes were on Aster, smiling pleasantly at her.

"How does one summon the Wolf, Mama?" Torenia asked.

Mama snapped her head Torenia's way with a scowl upon her face. The crow's feet at the corners of her eyes seemed sharper. "Careful, Torenia. Your question may have an answer you will fear."

"Please…" she tapered off, unable to go on.

Aster spoke up. "Yes, Mama—how?"

Mama sighed, relenting. "The man who wishes to summon the Wolf must sacrifice a daughter. Only then will he obey, devouring the bloodline commanded of him."

The young girls stared, wide-eyed. Aster's mouth was agape.

"Now, my girls, off to bed before the big bad wolf comes to steal you away!" She playfully raised her hands, fingers bent like the claws of a wolf, before standing and chasing her screaming daughters to their shared room. The girls leaped into their beds.

Huddled over Aster, Mama kissed her cheek. "Goodnight, my beautiful child. May good dreams find you."

Torenia waited for similar well wishes but knew she would never receive them. Mama rose from Aster's bed, walking to the big oak door without so much as a glance at her other daughter. Pursing her lips by the lantern, she blew out the flame.

1

THE YEAR OF THE RAVEN

Ten Years Later

Darkness crept around the edges of the room as the thick clouds covering the moon released an onslaught of snow. The inviting white fluff piled along the edges of the window. As it covered the small town of Silvania, silence fell over the world.

Within that silence, a voice no louder than the squeak of a mouse spoke. Lying on her stomach in the closet, Torenia clutched the small hand-held mirror. "Mirror, mirror on the wall, who's the fairest of them all?"

The mirror never replied, but in a lower voice—as though the mirror would be a man if awakened—she replied. "Torenia Luca is the fairest of them all."

Though Torenia's compulsion to hide away and study herself in the mirror was nothing new, it had recently changed. She dared not blink, watching as her reflection wavered, the light from the candle fluttering gently from her breath. Patience was something she had. Minutes crept by, her eyes growing tired and dry. When she was forced to blink, she did it slowly so as not to disturb the changes happening.

Her youthful face shifted; the reflection looking back at her in the mirror was hers, but different. More mature. Heart hammering, she held steady as she studied the face before her. It stared back at her, eyes narrowed slightly. A crook of a smile curled the corners of her lips. The wisp of a smile was not welcoming. It was hungry.

"Who *are* you?" Torenia whispered. But the face disappeared when she spoke, leaving her without answers, a vat of disappointment filling her chest.

Sighing, she put the mirror down on the floor and rested her head upon her arm. All her life, she had listened to her parents speak of how beautiful Aster was, how perfect she was. The daughter they had always wanted, so remarkable that none could be her equal in any regard. Her beauty could not be surpassed—the chestnut-colored hair that all Lucas had, paired with innocent brown eyes. The freckles that lightly dotted her round cheeks were perfectly placed, accenting her button nose.

Torenia was a different kind of beauty—one no one seemed to recognize. Her pale skin resembled her cousin Mihai, who had been cast out years before. She always worried that she would be next. Gingerly, to avoid making a noise that might wake anyone, she lifted the mirror again and looked at her reflection through piercing blue eyes.

"Torenia Luca is the fairest of them all," she confirmed this time and was satisfied.

She crawled out of the closet, the dark bedroom greeting her with the warm scent of cinnamon and must. Gentle breaths escaped her sleeping sister's lungs, the only noise in the house. The candle had been blown out before she vacated the cramped closet, the mirror tucked under an old rag where Aster would not find it. She took everything Torenia cherished.

Every night, it was the same—Torenia would lie as still as a petrified log until Aster's breathing softened, the gentle snores making her smirk. After an hour or so of waiting for Aster to fall into a deep sleep, Torenia would move at a snail's pace to avoid disturbing her sister.

And every morning was the same. Torenia would wake to the sound of Aster stomping her feet on the ground, yawning obnoxiously, even slamming the closet door in an attempt to wake Torenia. She was as cruel as she was pretty.

That morning was no different from the rest.

"Mama!" Aster never wasted an opportunity to catch Torenia doing wrong, to look bad in the eyes of their mother. "Torenia is still asleep, and she won't wake up! Perhaps she has caught an illness, we should send her away so I do not catch it!"

"I'm not ill, sister," Torenia hissed, yanking the down duvet over her head.

"No?" Aster yanked the duvet away. "If I were you, I would at least fake that I *was* ill if I looked like that. Your eyes look like they are rotting out of your skull."

In the darkness of the closet, Torenia didn't have enough light to see the black circles under her sleepless eyes. But in the light of the day, she knew they were obvious against her pale complexion.

"I am just tired, Aster," Torenia said. "And you yelling about it does not help me."

Aster leaned in. "Why would I help *you*?"

"Wretched girl." Torenia kicked the blanket off and maneuvered so fast that Aster bolted from the room in fear.

Alone at last, Torenia moved sluggishly towards the closet. After changing into her blouse, heavy skirts, and pinafore, she pinned back her long hair, hiding the silky black beneath a bonnet, before pulling on her winter boots. One quick glance out the window, still dark due to winter's grip, afforded her a glimpse of her reflection. A wicked grin appeared on her lips; she always looked prettier when she felt vicious.

"Torenia Luca is the fairest of them all." She stood taller, holding her head up high.

As she strolled confidently into the kitchen where Mother and Aster were baking, she smelled the herbs sprinkled in the dough. She longed for fresh bread, but chores had to be completed first. While Father went out early to butcher a chicken for the day's meals, it was Torenia's duty to milk the goats, collect the eggs, and feed the livestock.

"Wipe that grin off of your face, Torenia." Her mother stopped her before she could leave the house.

She did as she was told.

But Mama wasn't done, gripping Torenia's jaw and holding it firmly enough to leave marks. "With a smirk like that, you're going to get yourself defiled. Do you want that? Do you want to be known as the town *whore,* Torenia?"

Seeing that Aster was watching from the doorway of the kitchen, Torenia felt anger bubble up inside her like bile. Hot and sickening, it consumed her. She yanked away from her mother. "No, Mama."

"That's what I thought," she sneered. "Not that the boys in town would ever be attracted to the likes of you."

It was the Luca family's history of witchcraft and lycanthropy that made the townsfolk steer clear of them, but Mama's words still stung. Torenia bit back a retort and stormed out of the house. Her pace never slowed as she darted through the dead gardens in front of the house, round to the back where all the animals resided. The hard crunch of the night-old snow felt satisfying, like breaking a glass when she was angry. By the time she reached the goats, she had cooled off, though her cheeks still burned. As the animals scurried towards her, knowing she meant food, the relief of not being utterly alone swept over her.

After she collected the milk and the eggs, she sprinkled handfuls of grains for the chickens and hay for the goats. Tasks complete, she began the dreary trudge back home, where she would have to suffer through breakfast while they discussed Aster's latest accomplishments, sneering at her as they spoke of how many suitors their favored daughter would receive.

The crack of wood being split suddenly caught her attention. Torenia realized she had wandered off in her thoughts, taking a route along the fence that bordered their neighbor's property. Although she knew she would be punished for being late to breakfast, she walked towards the sound as it rang out again, drawing her in. She climbed onto the first rung of the fence that separated the two properties, standing tall so that she could survey the terrain before her.

In the distance, she spotted a young man about her age. He was chopping wood, shirtless, the sight making Torenia shiver. "You're going to freeze to death like that," she called to him.

Startled, he stopped mid-swing and glanced towards Torenia, wiping the sweat from his brow. He rested the ax over his broad shoulder before speaking. "What are you doing over this way?"

"I was curious about the noise." She gestured to the ax, watching in slight awe as he walked toward her. "What's your name?"

"I'm Adam." His tousled, sweaty hair was light brown, his eyes green. He reached the barrier between the two properties and held out his hand.

He seemed kind enough, so she took it. His firm grip was welcoming, but something else flickered as he held her hand longer than he should have. The thought came to her, similar to the voice from the mirror.

She would never hold a candle to Aster; why not become a witch and a whore?

2

_____

A fortnight passed. During that time, Torenia and Adam had done nothing but steal glances at one another during their morning chores as Torenia kept up with her detour along the fence. Each time she passed, he stopped chopping wood and looked her way. Though they spoke little, lust bloomed between them. The way his green eyes poured over her body, Torenia felt beautiful but, more importantly, powerful.

She had him in the palm of her hand, and she had done nothing to get it.

"Good morning, Adam." She spoke loud enough for him to hear, as he had not noticed her arrival at the fence that morning. Propped on top of the wooden fence, she broke the barrier between their homes, most of her body hanging over onto his family's side.

"To you as well, Torenia." His soft lips curled into a smile.

Adam leaned the ax against the woodpile and strolled with a confident swagger. Other than having shaken hands two weeks ago, they had not been this close. Something about this December morning was different; she could sense it. He positioned himself close, placing his hands on the fence on either side of her. Gentle snow danced around them, and, for a moment, only silence filled the gaps between the winter wind and the lone call of a raven.

"What brings you to this side of the fence?" he asked. "My father would frown upon a *Luca* on our property." The Luca name had been sullied due to the Wolf it was allegedly tethered to, even if most people scarcely believed the stories.

Torenia leaned forward so her nose was only an inch away from his. "All the more reason for me to be here. My father would tear me apart if he knew."

"Does the thrill *excite* you?" he asked. His left hand moved from the fence to her thigh, his grip firm through the soft fabric of her skirt.

Torenia grinned wickedly, the very look her mother hated. After all, if caving into this sensation made her wicked, then so be it. "Among other things."

Adam hesitated, and Torenia sensed it. He seemed unsure how to proceed, even with the hunger in her eyes encouraging him.

She grabbed his calloused hand and hitched up her heavy skirts, sliding his hand underneath them so that his skin rested against hers.

Removing her hand from his, Torenia walked her fingers up Adam's bare chest, sliding around to the back of his sweat-slick neck. Goosebumps prickled in the wake of her fingertips. Leaning towards him, she pressed her lips against his, tasting the sweat beading his upper lip. Before he even had the chance to kiss back, she pulled away, causing his grip on her thigh to tighten briefly.

"I am expected at home," Torenia teased. "Father will have my head if I show up late for breakfast again."

Adam's face tightened, but then he smirked. "We could kill him."

The thought had crossed her mind many times before, but Torenia didn't want him dead. Not to be with Adam, at least. He was fun for the time being, but he was just a boy. There were far more important things to her than boys. "Do you know somewhere warm we could meet tonight?" she whispered.

Adam understood her meaning; his hand slid out from under her skirts, placing it upon her cheek. "You must have put a spell on me with your beauty. I also would incur my father's wrath if I were caught in bed with a Luca."

"Tell me, Adam..." She paused, licking her lips. "Does the thrill *excite* you?"

The look in his eyes was answer enough.

Torenia pushed him aside so she could climb back to her side of the property line. She landed hard, sending flurries of snow into the frigid air as she hurried home. A thought lingered in her mind, planted like a seed, but the thrill of meeting Adam after dark excited her more than the thought of murder. Not her father; he was not the one she wanted to see lying bloody in the snow. It was Aster she wished to see dead. Torenia knew her sister was untouchable now, but she was happy to bide her time. She would fill it with all the things her mother had warned her against.

Picking up the bucket of milk and basket of eggs from where she had left them, she trudged home to suffer through another meal. The moment she stepped into the house, she was welcomed by the warmth of the wood stove and the cold glare of Mama.

"What took you so long, Torenia?" Her mother moved like a ghost, effortless and too fast. She yanked the bucket of milk from Torenia's hands, the metal handle cutting the bends of her fingers, and she began to bleed. "Perhaps Aster should take on your chores; at least then, we would be able to eat breakfast at a reasonable hour."

"Forgive me, Mama." Torenia moved swiftly to the kitchen with the basket of eggs, placing them on the table.

Mama's next command came sharply. "Make yourself useful and help your sister with the water."

Torenia did not miss the fact that *she* had returned from her chores before Aster but was still being punished.

Stepping outside in the winter chill again, Torenia approached Aster; she was not pulling heavy buckets of water out of the well but glancing towards the fence where Torenia had met Adam. An ominous feeling settled over her. She staggered for only a second, but it was long enough to shatter her brave façade.

"Arms too weak to pull up the bucket, sister?" Torenia taunted.

Aster turned with a dangerous look on her face. "I was just admiring the scenery."

"Trees and snow. Only a dull mind would admire the same sight we see every day." Torenia loved the trees and the snow, but she hated Aster and, therefore, anything she loved.

"Not *that,* you daft girl," Aster spat, staring down her older sister. "I saw a girl who looked remarkably like you, sister. She was being *touched* by that boy who lives over there."

Torenia knew the expression on her face resembled a brief shock, but she turned her nose up to banish it before sighing casually. "It is a shame you are already losing your mind, Aster. You would have made such a perfect wife. Perhaps we should keep you chained in the basement instead."

"What do you think father will do to you when he finds out you've lost your dignity to a farm boy?"

Torenia muttered under her breath, "My dignity has nothing to do with him."

"Mama would say otherwise."

Torenia lifted her skirts above the snow and crossed to where Aster stood, too fast for her little sister to evade. She grabbed Aster's pinned-back hair, yanking her head back. The shock in her sister's eyes gave her such pleasure that a grin spread across her lips. Although she was regarded as the black sheep of the family, she still had some power over Aster. Perhaps because she had less to lose.

"You saw nothing, Aster," Torenia warned, her grip tightening enough that the young girl whimpered. "Or I'll make sure you never see anything ever again."

The threat held, her younger sister nodding weakly, tears stinging her eyes. When Torenia released her, Aster fell forward, clutching the back of her head before quickly tucking her hair back underneath her cap. She watched pitifully as Torenia pulled up the bucket of water and strode back into the house with a confident gait, even though her hands shook.

3

T orenia's excitement over seeing Adam that night was tarnished
by Aster and the threat she posed. She did not, however, allow
this to completely derail her initial plans. For years, she had gotten
up in the middle of the night, crept silently into the closet, whispered
make-believe enchantments of beauty, and seen versions of herself in
the mirror that frightened her. Aster had never once woken up
before. This would be no different, except now Aster might be
expecting Torenia to sneak out.

Torenia had never despised sharing a room with Aster more than
she did that night as she waited for her sister to fall into a deep sleep.
She listened for her breathing to change for what felt like hours.
Would Adam still be there?

Having never crept out of the house, Torenia faced a new challenge entirely. She pulled a warm cloak from the closet, gingerly
draping it over her shoulders. Wrapped in warmth, she checked Aster
again, her deep breaths signaling she was sound asleep. Dim light
from the moon shone through the windows, coaxing Torenia out like
a moth to a flame in the darkness. She could feel the power it radiated, the same power the woods emitted.

Her boots were tucked away in a squeaky cupboard, so she was
forced to step barefoot into the snow. It hit her skin immediately, but

she hurried through gardens filled with nothing but winter flowers and empty boxes. Despite the cold, Torenia found beauty in being so close to nature; as soon as she was out of sight of the house, she twirled around like a dancer.

Pretending to be impervious to the cold, she made it to the fence before numbness consumed her toes. She scanned for any sign of Adam, her eyes catching sight of a light coming towards her, bobbing from side to side. Only when it drew closer did she see Adam behind the glare of the flame. The orange glow gave an ominous look to his strong features, the divot in his chin more defined.

"I'm so pleased to see you." Adam broke the silence, reaching out to help her climb the fence. He noticed her hands. "They're cut."

"I'm fine."

She smiled up at him to prove her statement as she hopped down. She was officially on his side of the fence, in forbidden territory, planning to act upon forbidden desires. Grinning through chattering teeth, she spoke again. "But I am freezing—tell me you have somewhere for us to go."

He glanced down at her feet, a puzzled expression on his face, quickly followed by a warm smile. He grabbed her, scooping her up into his arms playfully.

She gasped, then wrapped her arm around his neck for support.

He carried her through the snow, his steps heavy from the extra weight, shaking his head.

"I must be crazy, carrying a barefoot succubus through the snow, knowing I'd face lashings at the very least if we were to get caught."

"If everyone in this wretched town is sane, then I do not wish to be," she whispered.

The barn came into sight, the smell of hay tickling Torenia's nose. With her aid, Adam managed to open the door without putting her back down. A lantern hung along the wall, giving the inside of the barn a faint glow. No animals were within, only heaps of hay. A ladder led to a second-level loft overlooking the rest of the barn. Once inside, Adam set Torenia down and closed the door. His muscles flexed as he propped a bale of hay in front of the door so no one could get in.

Safe and secure, tension built between them. Torenia knew the other youths in the town were not impervious to the pull of sex; their bodies craved it. Their thoughts were only tarnished by their parents threatening that they would be taken away and offered to the maw of the Wolf. Torenia knew it was all lies—deceit to keep them obedient.

But the town needed change, and if it started with a rebellion of the youth, she was happy to be part of the upheaval. As they discarded their clothing and fell to the hay, she suddenly felt powerful. She pressed Adam back into the mound of hay, climbing atop him. The cuts on her hands left streaks of blood on his muscular chest as she pinned him to the ground. Adam did not appear to care about the mess she left on his skin as his hands went to her hips. Clunky, awkward movements, bursts of nervous laughter, and messy kisses enveloped them. Fingers trailed and explored—Torenia allowed her guard to fall as pleasure coursed through her veins.

Bliss swelled in the barn, filling it to the brim.

It did not last long, but both were satisfied, finally breaking through the wall their parents had erected to stop their children from having these cravings, Torenia wondered why they hid it from them. Why were adults so sour and bitter when this new feeling was so delicious? The thrill of defying them pleased her. But even better, she finally had something that Aster did not. Aster would never succumb to such impulses, she had her perfect reputation to protect. Torenia dressed quickly as the chill seeped back into the barn and under her skin.

Adam remained on the hay bales, unmoving for a time. "Why must you leave so soon?"

She raised an eyebrow, not expecting him to cling to her so quickly. "I cannot risk my sister waking and realizing I am gone."

He sighed, crossing his arms behind his head like a makeshift pillow. He met her eyes and smiled. "Will we meet again soon? I had fun."

She smirked. "I believe I can make it happen."

He rose to his feet suddenly, grabbing his trousers and stepping into them awkwardly. Panic lurked in his eyes as he gestured towards her abdomen. "You will not...get..."

Before he could fumble further, Torenia shook her head. "No, I will not."

"How can you be sure?"

"Women have been avoiding unwanted pregnancy since long before you and I were born," she assured him. She strode up to him and kissed him gently. "I will handle it."

4

Torenia's feet were numb by the time she made it to the single road that ran through town. Every rock and jagged piece of gravel dug into her feet, but she couldn't feel it. Her jaw was clenched tight, her arms wrapped around her. For the first time, she wished she was home under the warm covers.

One establishment always had its lights on and doors open, regardless of the hour. The two-story building was both a brothel and a tavern, built from sturdy logs far older than anyone could remember. The gentle serenade of a pan flute wrapped around Torenia, welcoming her into a strange building she had never considered entering. Standing before the large door, she felt a wave of confidence as she pushed it open and stepped inside. A few people glanced at her over their large pint glasses as a handful of pretty women seductively lolled their heads back, remaining seated on the laps of the men they were entertaining.

She was sure they could tell what she had done just by looking at her. But as quickly as people glanced her way, they returned to their own vices. It was both a relief and a slap in the face; she wanted people to be entranced by her. Standing just inside the doorway, she felt her confidence dry up. Just as she was about to turn and leave to head home and warm her frozen toes, a tall lady with frizzy red hair appeared. She had dark makeup around her eyes but a welcoming softness to her red-lipped smile.

"Young lady, your toes are going to fall off." The woman placed her hand on Torenia's shoulder and guided her toward the stairwell at the back of the tavern. As they walked, she continued to speak. "We'll get you warmed up. I'll see if I can find a pair of shoes the other girls have outgrown. What were you thinking, wandering about in the snow barefoot?"

"I, uhm..." Torenia wasn't used to speaking to adults who weren't her parents. And she certainly wasn't used to them being *kind*.

"Never you mind, it is none of my business." The woman opened a door when they reached the top of the stairs. "Go on, hop in."

Torenia eyed the bath, tendrils of steam coming off it, feeling its lull like a siren's call. She wondered if this woman always had a bath drawn or if she had known that Torenia was coming.

Curiously comfortable in the strange surroundings, Torenia peeled off her hay-scented clothing and slipped into the bath. Her toes burned at first, but it was worth the pain as the rest of her sunk into the hot water. She glanced at the woman as she handed her a bar of soap that smelled of apples mixed with rose petals. Not even her own mother treated her like this; experiencing the kindness now, she realized how much she craved it. From the day Aster was born, she was given attention and love, while Torenia was overlooked at best—ridiculed on good days, smacked on the bad. She coveted that attention now.

"What's your name, dear?" the woman asked, though the look in her eye told Torenia she already knew.

"Torenia Luca."

She smiled. "I am Madam Scarlett Răceanu."

Torenia had heard her name sneered at the dinner table occasionally. "This is your brothel?"

"Yes." Madam Scarlett went to a small closet and pulled out a perfectly folded towel. "When young ladies show up at my door, I offer them a roof over their heads, meals in their bellies, and protection—for a cost."

"I'm not here to become a..."

"A whore?" Madam Scarlett glanced at her. "No, of course not. You are too young. What are you, seventeen?"

Torenia offered a faint smile and nodded. "Girls far younger than seventeen work here."

"It is not a life I wish for them."

"And yet you—"

"Give them a place to stay, food to eat, and protection from the worst in this world. Does that make me a villain?"

Torenia pursed her lips tightly, unsure of what else to say.

Madam Scarlett smiled knowingly. "You're looking for something, correct?"

"I wish to avoid a pregnancy," she admitted, surprising herself with how easily she said the words.

Madam Scarlett did not look surprised. It was not uncommon in an establishment such as this, especially since it was the only place to go for miles around. "An easy request. Finish up here, and I will fetch what you need."

"I do not have any money," Torenia called before Madam Scarlett left the room.

"Oh, my dear, I would rather have one less unwanted child in this dreadful world than earn more money. I do not need your coin."

"Thank you," Torenia whispered.

After washing and drying herself off, Torenia slipped back into the clothes she had been wearing; they were still cold from the walk. Alone in the room, she looked around the small space. There was not much else there aside from the basin and a mirror that reflected her pale face back at her. She smiled; this version of her was different somehow. Running her fingers through her damp hair, she realized she was glowing. Her reflection was beautiful, and she was no longer ashamed of it.

Moments later, Madam Scarlett returned with a pouch made of leather. Closing the door behind her and shutting out the laughter, shouts, and moans of the brothel, she lifted her skirts a touch and walked over to Torenia. Pulling out a handful of what looked like crushed, white flower petals, she asked, "Is this the first time you've done this?"

Torenia nodded.

"Take this, and chew it slowly," she explained. "Do so once a day for the remainder of the week until this is empty."

"What is it?"

"*Daucus carota*; it will prevent pregnancy. It is not easy to come by."

"Why are you helping me?" Torenia held the bag close to her chest as she looked up at Madam Scarlett, searching her eyes for answers.

The older woman sighed, pushing back her frizzy hair, but it fell back over her face like a spring. Placing her hand on Torenia's shoulder, she explained. "When I was your age, something very bad happened to me. I was assaulted by my own brother. I was accused of seducing him and banished from my home. I became with child, and the infant was stillborn and deformed. Since then, I have never wanted any young woman to endure the horrors I did. I wanted to create a place where women have a say in what we do with our bodies and allow them to embrace carnal pleasures. We have more power than we are told, never forget that. You control your future, and if you ever need a safe place, you are welcome here."

Shocked but moved by her words, Torenia soaked in the wisdom. Everything Madam Scarlett said held so much weight, so much power behind it. Torenia wanted to grab hold of that power, to have it as her own. Her eyes darted up to Madam Scarlett's with a deep appreciation for this new knowledge and for the goal she now had.

The older woman grabbed Torenia's hands and squeezed them. "There are shoes at the door you may borrow. Return them when you are able."

Torenia nodded appreciatively.

"I must ask, dear; did you agree to what happened tonight?"

"I initiated it."

A smile spread across Madam Scarlett's red lips.

5

Home was in sight, and the cold had not yet dampened Torenia's demeanor. She walked with joyful tenacity, in a mood that would be hindered by nothing. In shoes one size too small, she arrived at the garden at the front of her family home. Her lids narrowed as she glared at the house; it might have been cold outside, but what lay inside the house was far colder. Careful not to make any noise, she slid off the shoes and tiptoed inside.

The heat of the dwindling fire in the hearth was no match for the warmth she felt within. Aside from Aster being smug and intrusive earlier, the day could not have gone better. Holding her shoes by the heels in one hand, Torenia used the faint glow of the fire and her other hand to guide her. Padding down the hall towards the bedroom, a smile still on her lips, she only noticed the faint flutter of candlelight from underneath the bedroom door when she reached the room.

A faint, unmistakable gleam danced in the small gap between the floor and the door. Torenia knew she had not left any candles burning; she knew her way through the bedroom in the pitch black all too well. When she had left to meet Adam, the house had been dark and silent except for the crackle of the fire. Aster must have woken sometime when Torenia was out and now was waiting until she returned.

Torenia had half a mind to go back to the brothel and agree to Madam Scarlett's terms. Maybe her mother was right; the Wolf would not come for her, but society would.

She stared at that light coming from the door as if challenging it.

Only one thought encouraged her to open it and enter the room; Aster had not woken her parents and told them of Torenia's doings. She was going to bargain. Taking a steely breath, she entered the small room to find Aster reading by lamplight. It was a familiar book, one Torenia had seen hundreds of times. It had no title, its ancient leather binding battered and well-used, the pages inside stained. A collection of stories and accounts of the cursed Wolf that haunted the town and the witchcraft that had started it.

Mama only read a few pages from it; she never allowed them to read about the witch and her craft. Witchcraft and adultery went hand-in-hand in her eyes; she only read cautionary tales written by men to make girls obedient.

Torenia had no doubt that her sister was reading the parts Mama kept hidden.

"Where have you been?" Aster sounded like Mama.

"What I've been doing is likely far less treacherous than what you are up to, sister," Torenia spat back.

"Reading is not forbidden to women anymore."

Torenia laughed, quiet but sharp. "You are not a woman. You are a child, Aster."

Aster closed the book slowly, her eyes edging underneath Torenia's skin like knives. Even though she was younger, she held the advantage when it came to their parents. They had always loved Aster more; Torenia knew that if they had to choose to save one of their lives, it would be her sister. It ate away at her when she was younger to know that she was first born but second best. Now, however, Torenia had something that Aster didn't—a sense of freedom.

Aster put the book on the end of the bed and slipped out, her off-white nightgown reaching her ankles. Face-to-face in the small bedroom, one would hardly have known they were sisters; where Aster had a soft chin and a button nose, Torenia was sharp with a defined jaw. Aster was far shorter than Torenia, yet she sized her up without any fear in her eyes, smirking.

"I thought something odd was happening when you were late for breakfast. When I confronted you earlier, you were very defensive." Aster obviously had a speech prepared. "Knowing that something was not quite right, I decided to feign being asleep until I could catch you sneaking out again—"

"Again? I have never snuck out before, brat."

"Oh, do not bother lying, Torenia," she hissed. "Ever since we were children, I would wake, and you would be nowhere to be found."

"I was in the closet." Torenia shook her head and rolled her eyes as she tried to figure out Aster's angle.

"Not tonight, you weren't."

"No." Torenia knew she couldn't lie her way out of this one, but negotiation was still on the table. "Do you want to know what I was doing?"

Aster nodded, so Torenia leaned in close as though to whisper a secret shared only by sisters. When she had her undivided attention, she shoved her aside and grabbed the large book. It felt heavy and powerful in her grasp, and she had half a mind to swing it at Aster's skull. She wondered if it would break her neck if she put enough strength into it.

"First, I want to know what *you* were doing," Torenia chided, holding the book above her head.

As Aster reached for it, she realized that the age barrier was coming into play. She wouldn't win a physical fight. "Light reading." Aster sneered as she spoke. "Reading about what will happen to you now that you've become a whore."

Torenia laughed. "You still believe those silly tales?"

Aster just scowled.

A dog-eared page drew Torenia's attention, her eyes poring over the script. They were difficult to decipher, but she managed. She read the words aloud. "*I have discovered a brew that will peacefully kill anyone who drinks more than two drops. The potency of it comes from the mushroom'*—"

31

Aster reached for the book again, disrupting Torenia.

Torenia smirked. "Were you going to use this little potion on me then, Aster?"

"It was far too peaceful for you. If I wanted you dead, I'd use something more practical."

"Witchcraft. Now, Aster, that is even worse than what you think I've done." She wished she had thought of it first; the secrets to the Craft had been right before her this whole time. All she had to do was steal the book. However, she knew if caught with it, she would be cast out or burned on a pyre; Aster would be scolded at best. Torenia closed the book and held it behind her back. "So, we both have a secret; what will we do about it?"

For the first time in her life, Aster appeared to truly consider Torenia's words. Like she was tasting something new for the first time, she moved it around her mouth before frowning. Her scowl made her look ugly, Torenia noted. When she scowled, she still looked striking.

When Aster finally made her decision, she reached out a steady hand. "I won't tell Mama and Papa if you won't."

"We ignore each other's business," Torenia added.

Aster rolled her eyes. "Deal."

6

The cusp of spring brought a slight warmth during the day, but the bone-deep chill at night remained. The moon beamed down from a cloudless sky, the threat of further snow averted. However, the paths remained covered. Over time, they'd become packed down, creating sheets of ice that were warped and pitted. Torenia's boots crunched on it as she slipped along, arms out to keep herself steady. There was little light to guide her as she walked toward the brothel, but she knew the path with her eyes closed.

She had left the house in a hurry; the tension was too much to handle. Aster had grown more disturbed each day, whispering incantations and incoherent speech whenever Torenia was in their bedroom. It seemed like a charade, but Torenia would not risk her life. Every night she planned to see Adam, she felt Aster's watchful eyes boring into her and would slink back under the blankets. It was as if Aster had found a spell never to sleep again so she could spy for their parents. Torenia couldn't help but wonder if Aster was pretending, as she had yet to see her *do* anything resembling the Craft, but even if she was just biding her time to make sure Torenia got caught red-handed, she had to be careful.

Only two months in, and their deal hung by a fine thread, threatening to snap at any time. Though they had agreed to mind each other's business and not tell their parents what the other was up to, Torenia couldn't trust Aster's word. She knew that if their parents were to discover what Aster was doing, Mama would likely scold her younger sister and nothing more. But even Aster knew that Father would take witchcraft far more seriously.

Torenia told her parents she was helping people in town, the elderly who struggled to go to the market and the sick who couldn't get out of bed. She was out of the schoolhouse and waiting for her father to marry her to an acceptable suitor. No one wanted to marry a Luca girl, let alone Torenia, with her pale skin and coal-black hair. It stung, but she would never let it show. There was one place, however, where she was always accepted.

Music and laughter welcomed her when she opened the brothel doors. A smile crossed her face; this was home, more so than the house where she was born and raised. Warmth hugged her as she walked inside. It was the dead of winter when she had first scurried in here, barefoot and frozen. Spring neared at last, and she was a familiar face at the establishment.

"Good evening, Torenia!" Elena, a striking woman of similar age to Torenia, shouted from atop a man's lap. She had slung her arms around his neck and now leaned back, her breasts spilling from the loosely tied corset binding them.

From the back of the room, Madam Scarlett made her presence known. Her fearlessness gained her respect, and she possessed an authoritative demeanor that ensured no man stepped out of line when it came to the brothel women, for her birds were sacred. Scarlett Răceanu was the only person Torenia truly felt safe with, and she visited as often as she could sneak out. Madam Scarlett was also the only person she trusted regarding her current trouble with Aster.

"Torenia, it has been too long." Scarlett leaned down and kissed Torenia on each cheek, leaving faint shadows of red lipstick on her skin.

"I have been growing my own garden," Torenia admitted. Though she rarely saw Adam, she still needed to protect herself. "Though I have used other methods as well."

"That does not mean you are not welcome here if just to show your face."

"I must ask you something privately." Torenia's face fell slightly.

Madam Scarlett nodded, quickly scanning the room to ensure all her birds were safe. She grabbed Torenia's hand and led her up the stairs. Moans penetrated the walls, which had once made Torenia blush. She smiled now; this was a place of indulgence and happiness. Those values were sacred within these walls, no matter what the townsfolk said.

Inside Madam Scarlett's room, the quiet settled. Scarlett walked to the window where a metal bird cage sat and reached inside with her slender hand to grab the bird within. Small, with a gray coat and some patches of black, the dove stepped gingerly onto Scarlett's hand and cooed gently.

"What concerns you, little bird?" she asked Torenia.

"I am not one of your birds," Torenia reminded her.

"Oh, my dear, you are." Scarlett acted as though she were speaking to the dove and not Torenia. "You may not spread your legs for the patrons here, but you keep me company, bringing joy to my life like a daughter might, and I would do anything to protect you from harm."

Part of Torenia wondered if this was how Scarlett got her birds. Did she sweet-talk all of them, making them feel like her brothel was a better home than the ones they were raised in? It was not a bad thing, the way Madam Scarlett kept people close, but it was not the life that Torenia sought. She wanted out of this town but needed more than the clothes on her back to do that.

"My troubles bloom from my sister," she admitted. She paused to consider what was safe to reveal, nibbling her lip. "She knows my secret, but she hangs it over my head as a threat."

"But she has not informed your parents? What is she scared of?"

Torenia walked over to the desk below the other window. Her fingers numbly pushed through the papers on the desk, eyes staring at her reflection in the dark window. She had aged noticeably in the last few months, or perhaps she simply told herself such things. She recently turned eighteen years of age and wondered when her father might decide to marry her off. The thought repulsed her.

"I caught her studying something...something dark and forbidden." Torenia turned to look at Madam Scarlett, who stood to the side, stroking the dove's little puffed-out chest. Torenia continued, her voice cautious. "Witchcraft."

"A true Luca." Scarlett finally looked at Torenia, her eyes sharp; she was considering something. "Would you like to learn more than her?"

Torenia wondered if this meant Scarlett was a witch. "Is it not forbidden to practice witchcraft?"

"Everything in this building is forbidden." Scarlett rose and walked right up to Torenia, stroking her pale cheek. "That which is forbidden is not always bad. Tell me, Torenia, when you sneak into the blacksmith's barn with his son, do you feel you are doing a bad thing? When you come to me to avoid being with child, do you feel like a bad person? When you *indulge,* do you feel bad?"

"I do not *feel* bad; however, I do feel as though I have *done* something bad."

"This is because you have not been taught that sometimes the 'bad thing' is truly good." Scarlett removed her hand from Torenia's cheek and opened the window, releasing the dove, before muttering something in an unfamiliar language to Torenia. After a moment, she spoke again. "I am learned in the arts of witchcraft, Torenia. Does this scare you?"

"I am not sure." In truth, she was shaking with excitement as, with a teacher, she could learn what Aster could never achieve with one book.

"What does your heart tell you?"

"My heart tells me nothing of importance. My mind tells me I need to remain one step ahead of Aster before she gets me killed," Torenia said, unsure where the words had come from.

"Spoken like a true witch."

7

S pring came with a second onslaught of snow. It refused to ebb,
littering the town with a fresh batch of powder every other
night. The town began to grow wary and worried about the cold. The
spring flowers refused to sprout, the snow blanketing the fields and
preventing crops from being planted. The screams of animals echoed
throughout the town as livestock were slaughtered, there being too
little to feed them. The sound was a brutal melody that filled the air
every morning.

These cries reinforced why Torenia needed Scarlett's instruction.
In recent weeks, learning about the types of magic had ensnared her,
the forbidden knowledge expanding her mind. Every living thing was
intertwined with the earth below, and it was from that earth that she
gained her power. Every drop of blood spilled enhanced the magic of
the trees and soil; this was a much more sinister magic than Aster
learned from her book, for it was blood magic.

The screams of the cows and pigs, chickens and goats disappeared once she was behind the heavy doors. The brothel was quiet
in the morning, the disheveled main room resembling a drunk's
hangover. Chairs were askew, half-empty glasses sitting on tables, the
odd garter or shoe left on the ground or draped over a door handle.

Men and women slept behind closed doors, the men who remained too scared to return home to their wives.

Entering the room where Scarlett taught Torenia the Craft day after day, she was startled at the carnage before her eyes. A raven, as black as night, flopped on the ground, its wing broken but mendable. Blood seeped from the wound, making its feathers look slick with oil. Scarlett sat, eyes fixed on the raven, murmuring something under her breath. She did not even notice Torenia walking in, she was so focused on the bird in front of her.

"What happened to it?" Torenia asked, her voice barely a whisper.

Scarlett's head snapped up, her eyes entranced and clouded. When they returned to their normal color, she realized Torenia was there. "Her. What happened to her."

"What happened to her?"

"She was attacked by a man." Scarlett's brow furrowed as she spoke. "Come, listen to what she has to say."

Torenia stepped around the raven and followed Scarlett's instructions. She placed a hand on its breast, searching for the pain and fear. She repeated the incantation word for word as Scarlett recited it for her. Suddenly, she felt the raven's pain as it shot through her veins; her whole body tensed, her back arching at a grotesque angle. A shriek ripped from her lips, her body frozen in agony. Slowly, the pain withered but still lingered, and a vision emerged.

The raven dropped effortlessly, floating down onto the farmer's garden post. Once a tree, it felt foreign to her talons. She hopped down and pecked at the dirt, searching. Hungry, so hungry. Loud noises disrupted her, and she hopped back as Man attacked her. She could not escape, a barrier of manmade material holding her within the garden. Something shiny slashed at her as he neared, and in her panic, she flew into the barrier. It tangled around her, but as Man slashed again, a hole opened and freed her. Blood. Blood fell from her body as she flew, only to collapse to the earth. That is when Woman found her.

Torenia gasped, ripped from the connection, her body able to move freely again. She whipped her head around to look at Madam Scarlett. "What can we do for her?"

"We can mend her wounds; this is a task you must complete.

Form a bond with her, trust her, and she will trust you. Then..." Scarlett's voice faded, and she slid a book over to Torenia.

"Then she might accept my request to become my familiar." Torenia realized, finishing the other woman's sentence. Her first attempt at blood magic. Earth magic guided all witches, but blood magic made them into what the world feared. Although not all familiars were created in the same way, for each witch was vastly different from the next, creating one through blood magic was the strongest way.

Madam Scarlett's familiar was the dove, small and unnoticed when it sat upon windowsills and listened in. Some people even left out seeds for it, opening windows in the warmer months, unknowingly letting Scarlett listen in to every secret they possessed. Birds were the ideal familiar, as they went completely unnoticed when lingering close to a house. They could cover long distances. They could see everything. Madam Scarlett had explained that some were drawn to cats, rats, and even foxes, but these were often killed by people who did not want them too close to their homes. Birds were inconspicuous and safe.

Immediately, Torenia knew that she wanted this beautiful raven as her familiar, to remain by her side through thick and thin. Though the bird was large and would be spotted more easily, she fell instantly in love. Without any more guidance from Madam Scarlett, she began to tend to the large bird. It flopped, trying to get away from her, but after some gentle coaxing, they began to understand one another.

Hours passed, and Madam Scarlett came and went from the room, mostly leaving Torenia and the raven on their own. Over the last few months, she had taught Torenia so much that she trusted that the well-being of the raven was in good hands. When the raven was strong enough, Torenia knew she would need guidance on how to make the bird her familiar. The bond was not difficult, but it was everlasting—to do it properly was vital.

Slowly, the day turned to night, but Torenia did not notice, forgetting that she was supposed to meet Adam. There were more important things than boys. When the raven finally fell into a light sleep, with the encouragement of an herbal tincture, Torenia sat back on the floor and wiped the sweat from her brow. Blood was smeared over her pale features; she could smell it, the sharpness of it upon her tongue. Glancing out the window, she saw that it was night and finally thought of Adam but felt a wave of serenity wash over her. By the end of this, no matter how dirty her hands were, she would have a familiar, which was worth more than ten of him.

She saw how love and lust became mixed up in the home and the brothel; though she cared for Adam, she knew he would not become her husband. Maybe no one would. Erasing these thoughts from her mind, she turned her attention back to the raven as it stirred. Her knees ached from spending hours on the wood floor tending to the bird, but she couldn't bring herself to stand.

"Stronger connection," she mumbled, wishing Scarlett could guide her more as she pulled from the chasm of knowledge she had learned within these walls. She grabbed a blade, already covered in blood and feathers, and wiped it on her skirt. It easily sliced her palm, blood oozing out hot and red. Reading the words of the pages once more, she pressed her palm to the raven's wound.

Animam meam do vobis: Ego tibi dabo vos ad me. Her voice came out as a hiss. The window jerked open; the wind blew in snow, swirling around the room like magic. "*Te vivere, ut ministrent mihi, et ego ad te defendat.*"

The wind that whipped through the room wrapped around Torenia, yet she did not feel the slightest inkling of cold. Under her clothing, caressing her, she felt it inside of her. Even though she was shocked by this magic, she embraced it, welcomed it, felt honored by it. Then it left, taking a piece of her, something now missing inside of her. A single white orb glowed, falling through the swirling snow. It floated gracefully down, hovering over the raven before sinking into the feathers and flesh.

The eyes of the raven flew open, but it did not appear startled or in any pain.

"Rahella." Torenia gave the raven her name. "You are Rahella."

The door opened, and Madam Scarlett walked in. If she was impressed, she did not show it as she studied the raven. "You should see what she is capable of."

"She is still wounded," Torenia reminded her. She felt such a strong connection to Rahella, a love that she had not felt for anyone, or anything, before.

"You healed her when you gave her part of your life." Madam Scarlett knelt beside Torenia as she spoke. "Welcome to the world, Rahella."

Torenia raised a brow, fueled by her success. She wanted to know what poor Adam had done when she never showed up. "Go find Adam."

8

V ein-like paths weaved around the houses and farms below her. Pure white snow piled up, covering more and more of the tracks left behind from the day. Plumes of smoke rose from each house, fouling the air with the stench of burning cedar. Burning the very trees that once housed so many creatures. Just as nature did not care for man, man did not care for nature.

Flying west, Rahella expanded her wings as she glided, the bitter air lashing at her, dense feathers protecting her from the cold. The house came into sight as she pulled her mended wings into her sides and dove. When the earth came up at her, threatening and fast, she fanned out her trustworthy wings again and swooped with grace. Her keen eyes scoured for anything, anything at all.

And then, a scream. Ear piercing, but not threatening. Rahella flew towards the sound. A barn stood tall, and she neared it nervously. Humans had not been kind to her, especially of late. Landing on the pommel of a shovel and standing up from the dirt, she peered around to look within the barn. Doors shut, she could not spy, so she hoisted her body back up into the air, flying around in search of a window. There were many, and when she landed, she saw everything.

The ugly color of naked flesh, uncovered by fur or feathers. Legs tangled, hands groping, hair matted and covered in hay. Man—Adam—

atop, Woman below. Rahella cocked her head to the side, trying to get a better look at who was below the Adam that Torenia sought. She had felt the same feelings as Torenia when she gave her part of her life. And so, when Woman turned to look at the raven, making bold eye contact with her, Rahella was seared with pain. Though she did not understand why, she had an ache deep inside her chest as she saw enough to return to Torenia.

She lifted again, her giant wings causing small tornados, as she twisted her body through the air and returned to her witch.

The pain of ripping herself out of the connection with Rahella made Torenia shriek, her bones rippling as she straightened. The joints snapped back when she broke the connection, and she was rendered mute for a moment. Scarlett sat across from her, legs crossed, hands on her lap. A burning anger filled Torenia's chest, though it only showed as she tightened her hands into fists, squeezing until her nails dug into her palms, stopping before they could break her flesh.

"What did you see?" Scarlett asked.

"Betrayal," she replied, making eye contact with the older woman.

"Behind every strong witch is betrayal. Betrayal of a man."

"Like your brother?"

Scarlett flinched, nodding.

"And what did you do to your brother?"

"I fled; I was terrified."

"You have never gone back to take your revenge?"

She shook her head. "Revenge can lead to very bad things, Torenia. My revenge is my success. My survival."

Torenia frowned, unhappy with her discovery. She wanted Aster dead, and she wanted Adam to see how he had hurt her. *Don't let them see your weakness,* she thought. He was just a boy; surely, he did not have the power to hurt her. Yet he had. He had cut her deep.

"I should return home," Torenia said as she rose. Her hands smoothed out the wrinkles of her skirt as she walked to the window where Rahella was perched, tending to the freshly healed wound. The raven stepped quickly onto Torenia's arm.

"She must not be seen as yours; people will begin to suspect what you have dipped your hands into, and they will come for you," Scarlett warned. "A familiar can be the greatest asset a witch can have, but her quickest downfall as well."

Torenia left with Scarlett's imparted wisdom fresh in her mind. The moment she stepped outside of the brothel, she let Rahella use her newly healed wings, knowing she would return when she called for her. Months before, she had walked to the brothel, worried about pregnancy but confident because she had become a woman. Now she left the brothel with her shoulders back and head held high, a different kind of power filling her. That energy ran through her veins, and she could not wait to bring Aster down.

The barn was in sight. Light glowed inside, and Torenia knew that Aster and Adam were still there, waiting for her; at least Aster was. With a gentle stride and a wicked grin, Torenia opened the doors and caught them lying in the hay, a small blanket shielding their bare skin. Adam looked shocked, pulling the blanket higher. Aster smiled. She knew Torenia would find out one day; she had wanted her to.

"Torenia!" Adam exclaimed. "I...I was..."

"You don't need to explain yourself, Adam." Torenia flashed him a smile dripping with poison. "My sister has to have everything that means something to me; she would have found a way to win you from me eventually. I am disappointed, however, that you caved so soon."

Adam stood, stunned.

Aster rose to her feet, flaunting her young beauty. Dressing herself quickly, she pulled a few strands of hay from her hair and cleared her throat. Pretending Torenia was not in the barn with them, she turned her attention to Adam, pursing her lips. "I suspect there will be some family turmoil ahead, Adam. If I were you, I would keep your distance."

He nodded, stepping into his trousers and sliding his shirt over his bulky shoulders before scurrying from the barn with reddening cheeks. Torenia didn't bother trying to stop him; he had made his choice and, just like everyone else, had chosen Aster over her. Trying not to let the anger and embarrassment show through her expression, she directed her attention back to Aster.

"Shall I escort you home, sister? Or are you too old for an escort now that you've had sex with the blacksmith's son?"

"I would fancy a walk with you, Torenia."

A fiery stare-down between the sisters heated the air around them before Aster walked up to Torenia, wrapping her arm around her sister's. Arm-in-arm, they left the barn, but not before Torenia kicked over one of the candles. The wax leaked, the flames spreading and catching the hay quickly.

"You are wicked, sister. There was no need to bring him into this."

"You're the one who brought him into this," Torenia snapped back, clutching Aster's small bicep with her other hand. She would be bruised, but she would not be able to complain to Mama or Father, not without explaining where she had been. Even Aster wouldn't weasel her way out of that so easily.

As they walked toward home, they heard shouts coming from Adam's property. Two men roared, and a woman screamed. Flames had engulfed the whole barn, the crackle of the fire snapping as smoke filled the sky, permeating the cold winter air. Torenia breathed it in like it was freedom.

"Now I know you try to hurt me any way you can. You turned our parents against me many years ago. You have dabbled in witchcraft, but I must tell you, sister, that you have entered a fight that you cannot win," she began. "You are self-taught—admirable but foolish. A single book cannot teach you everything. You whisper mindless incantations and fawn over potions you will never brew. You need a mentor, or you will go nowhere."

"And who might that be? You?" Aster laughed.

"I would not be your mentor if the only other option was to have my feet sawed off. No, I have a mentor, and she has taught me what you could not even dream to learn," Torenia warned, then called to Rahella while releasing her death grip on her sister. The raven swooped out of nowhere, black on black in the night sky, landing on Torenia's extended arm. "Should you continue this path of witchcraft, I will have Rahella tear your pretty brown eyes out of their sockets. Then I will cut out your heart and feed it to her."

"You...You have a familiar? How?" Aster stopped dead in her tracks.

"As I've said, without a mentor, you can learn nothing but superficial spells and potions." Torenia sighed. "I know you wish me dead, but you cannot accomplish this with witchcraft."

Aster paused, collecting herself after the initial shock that Torenia had gained a familiar. As usual, she was one step ahead despite Torenia's scramble to do the same.

"I do not need to accomplish it with witchcraft, sister." Aster smiled menacingly, from ear to ear. "This is why I have informed Mama that you have been whoring yourself out at Madam Scarlett's brothel. There are eyewitnesses, and who do you think they will believe when they find the obvious evidence of witchcraft in our bedroom? Me? Or the child they never wanted? A witch *and* a whore, just think of what they will do to you. And your mentor."

Torenia gasped. The lights were on in the house, the flames of the lanterns flickering and dancing. She knew that her parents were waiting, they had likely stumbled upon the witchcraft in the room—all belonging to Aster. She had led them right to it, the conniving child she was. Of course, they would believe she had found it, explaining that Torenia had been up to no good, that she had been sneaking out to spend nights with the boy next door.

Torenia knew she could not run, so she whispered, "Rahella, warn Scarlett."

9

With shaking hands and steady feet, Torenia entered the house to face her family's fury. The door was wide open when Aster shoved Torenia inside, her body language changing. A gasp came from Torenia's lips as she braced herself for the floor. Catching herself before she hit the ground full force, her wrists stung from the impact.

Before her, on the floor, was the book. A satchel of herbs and mushrooms was scattered beside it, their dried aroma subtle. Torenia was able to grab the one item in that pile that was hers—the small handheld mirror she used to whisper to in the dead of night. She tucked it beneath the cinched waist of her skirt as Aster's sharp voice filled the room.

"I found her, Mama. I...I just knew she was sneaking out. I found her with the neighbor boy. I also saw her practicing... Oh, I cannot speak the words!" Aster's voice sounded false in Torenia's ringing ears.

"Get away from her, Aster! She may lash out with her dark magic!" Their mother beckoned for Aster to come closer, glaring at Torenia with a cruelness that was all too familiar.

Aster scurried to her and was wrapped in Mama's seemingly warm and welcoming arms. Torenia could not remember the last time anyone held her in their arms like that; she was never embraced. As she clambered to her knees, as tall and strong as she could be in the face of blame, Mama leaned forward and slapped her hard. She winced but remained upright, hand pressed to her side where the mirror was nestled. Blood dribbled down her lip; she darted her tongue out to taste it.

"I will not have a witch in my house nor a whore," Father snarled, his arms crossed.

"We come from a family known for treachery, deceit, and witchcraft," Torenia spat. "You would do well to kick out both your daughters."

"What have you done to her?" her mother shrieked, clutching Aster. "How dare you influence her in your dark arts!"

"We are Lucas. It's in our veins." Torenia leaned forward, smiling through her words, the blood smeared over her chin, making her look like a creature of legends.

"That's enough," Father said, grabbing Torenia by the collar of her dress. Instinctively, she reached up and clawed at his hand, but he paid no mind. She choked as he dragged her, throwing her out of the house and into the snow. He stomped outside and grabbed her hair this time, yanking her along the path.

"Father, wait!" Aster broke from her mother's hold and ran into the cold. "She has a mentor, another witch, the whore Scarlett..."

Her father's face went red as the blood on Torenia's chin. Something in the way his brows furrowed and his lips pressed tight together made her go cold. She began to shout in protest; it did not matter what happened to her, but she could not bring Scarlett into this, not after everything she had done for her. She fought her father's grasp, but he did not care. She screamed, pleading, calling for help.

As Father dragged her through the muddy streets, Mama and Aster hurried along behind them. Torenia was only able to catch glimpses of them through her tear-filled eyes. Mama's face was pinched, but her eyes were alight with malicious excitement. Aster did nothing to hide her beatific joy, sneering whenever she locked eyes with Torenia.

Father dropped her in the center of the street before the brothel.

She collapsed into the snow; a wretched sob shook through her. Her scalp screamed in pain, and her throat was already bruising from his grip. The slap Mama had delivered had been sharp, like her, but did not linger like the damage Father inflicted.

"Scarlett!" Father shouted.

Father stormed up to the brothel doors, banging his fists against the wood. He walked back down the steps and gripped Torenia's hair again while he waited for Scarlett to emerge. Behind them, the townspeople gathered to see what the commotion was about.

Madam Scarlett pushed open the door and glared viciously down at Torenia's father from the top of the stairs. "Good evening, Mr. Luca. Come for my services?" she asked. "Again?"

Torenia's head was spinning, but she looked up at Scarlett. *What does she mean by again?*

"You have tainted my daughter, witch." He pointed the gun at her.

The townsfolk murmured amongst each other. Most of them were glad to have something to talk about, somewhere to point the finger when the next thing went wrong. The Luca family already had a stain upon their name, but now there was a scandal.

"Was giving your daughter a roof over her head, meals in her belly, and a warm fire to thaw the ice you put inside of her considered tainting her? If she learned anything from me, it was that she does not need you or your wife to keep her safe." She looked at Torenia's mother and sister in the crowd with disappointment. "I have taught her nothing but survival, something you forced her to learn in the cruelest of ways." Scarlett took one more step closer.

"That is all part of your trickery, to make young girls think you care about them and then force them to sell their bodies." He stood stock still.

"Torenia has done nothing of the sort; she has simply come to me for safety from people like you."

Father muttered something under his breath; only Torenia heard. "I will hear no more of this."

Turning towards the townspeople, he raised his hands. "We have a witch in our midst. She has corrupted your daughters, your sisters. She has been hiding in plain sight, and we have let this whore get away with it for too long! I have proof now of her witchcraft, for she has corrupted my daughter! We must put an end to this and make an example of them both!"

The crowd erupted into a frenzy. Someone threw a rock, and it struck Scarlett. Blood spilled lazily from the wound upon her cheek. She didn't bother to wipe it away.

"Stop!" Scarlett shouted, her voice full of fury. "You will not harm your child. I am a witch, yes, and I have been feeding into her curiosity, but she has not learned anything of the Craft. Everything she has done that seems suspicious, I have forced her to do it. She does not know the difference between reality and my trickery. I am to blame, and I will accept my consequences."

"That is confession enough." Torenia's father grabbed Torenia again, this time by the shoulder, and walked up the steps toward Scarlett.

"She's lying!" Torenia shrieked, tears streaming down her face. "She's lying!"

"Quiet now, little bird," Scarlett said softly. Then she addressed Torenia's father. "This is how you repay me for keeping your secrets?"

"I could have had you killed any time in the past seventeen years, Scarlett."

"Had you any decency, you would have let us raise her," Scarlett said. "Lilith may have died in childbirth, but my Birds care for one another better than any Luca ever could."

"Scarlett," Torenia said, "what are you talking about?"

"Your mother was a Bird, Torenia."

"Enough!" Father said. He looked back at the crowd. "The witch must pay for her crimes."

"No!" Torenia shrieked, yanking away from her father's hold and scurrying towards Scarlett.

The older woman helped Torenia to her feet and clutched her chin. She whispered in her ear. "Run far away from here."

Before Torenia could reply, Scarlett pressed her bright red lips to Torenia's forehead. Then she pulled back and stepped down the stairs to the snowy road as another rock struck Scarlett. Torenia rushed after her, but Rahella swooped in and flapped her giant wings to stop her. She fell into the snow. The bird would not let her approach the fury of the townspeople.

She scrambled to her feet, the attention of the town now entirely on Scarlett. Slurs spewed from their mouths, filling the air with a chorus of profanity. Silvania had not killed a witch in Torenia's lifetime, and they were hungry for it. Forced by her own fear to watch as they began plucking stones from the ground, Torenia could only shake where she stood.

Chairs were taken from the brothel as wood for fuel, and then the flame appeared in the distance. It all felt surreal as a man handed Father a torch, the bright light shining like the sun on the darkest of days. How many of the men participating had spent nights at the brothel? Torenia wished never to see such fury or hatred ever again.

"We protect this town!" he shouted, and everyone cheered. It was the first time the whole town agreed on something; they had a common enemy. "Witches and whores have no place here; let us make sure that they never forget. Should any more daughters turn to the Craft, they will remember this day. The day the Lucas put an end to it!"

Father struck Scarlett, sending her to her knees. Those who picked their weapons from the earth began to throw them with unbridled wrath. Scarlett shouted as some of the bigger ones made contact, the thud of stone against flesh sickening. Amidst the horrors, Aster stood tall, more confident than Torenia had ever been. With a smile that grew ten times wider as Scarlett crumpled, Aster showed how truly vile she was.

Torenia covered her ears when she heard the first bone break, but it did not drown out the scream it drew from Scarlett. Forcing herself to watch, she felt sobs rake through her body; she had no control over herself. The cheers of everyone in the town were not loud enough to cover the shrill sound from Scarlett. Her screams turned into whimpers and then dull moans.

It was all over in minutes, but it felt like days. Exhaustion filled Torenia, but there was no time to waste.

She was next.

10

Scarlett's body was nothing more than a heap of broken bones and blood-stained clothing. The sight turned Torenia's stomach. She let out one shuddering breath and then swallowed; her mouth was dry.

"What about that one?" A man in the crowd pointed at Torenia, freezing and numb in the snow.

"She has brought shame into this family, but she is my daughter," Father said, though it was not quite merciful.

Father turned and addressed the crowd. "Go gather your children, your daughters and wives. I want everyone to see what happens here tonight. Remember this night as the night the Luca family made a sacrifice for the best interest of Silvania!"

A gentle nudge reminded Torenia that she was still alive, for now. Rahella pressed her sharp beak against her arm. Shaking but determined, she pushed herself from the ground, rising to her feet. Facing her family, each of them glaring at her, she shook her head. Her father, the liar, who had a child with a Bird, her false mother, who despised her, and her half-sister, who loved to be cruel. *I owe them nothing,* Torenia thought. *Especially not my life.*

"You will not have me this night," she said. "And you will pay for what you have done here."

"Torenia, you have been corrupted; you must pay for what you have done. There is no other way to wash your hands of the blood upon them," her mother told her, glancing at Aster, who gave a single nod. The malice in their mother's eyes told Torenia that she knew. She knew about Aster, what she had done—they would keep this secret from Father all their lives. She wanted her dead to protect Aster's image. There was nothing that she could do to change the opinion her family had of her, so she had to break the bond.

"No," Torenia said firmly, then turned her back on her family.

The townspeople were beginning to file back into the streets with their tired wives and daughters in tow. Everyone's eyes bore into her as Torenia climbed the stairs to the tavern and disappeared inside. The confident way she walked stunned the crowd, leaving them wondering what she would do next. The moment she was inside, though, Torenia ran as fast as she could to Scarlett's room.

She gathered everything she would need for a journey, throwing a few books, some potion bottles, a necklace she could sell, and a blanket into a satchel, then draped a cloak over her shoulders. "This might not be enough to get me to the next town," she said to herself, looking at the meager supplies she'd gathered. "I don't even know where Silvania ends, but I can't stay here."

There was no time to grab food, but she pocketed a half-finished bottle of whiskey, knowing it would keep her warm. Footsteps came up the stairs. Down the hall, a door banged open, its hinges groaning, the wall shaking as the handle hit it. One of Scarlett's birds screamed. *This is it,* Torenia thought. *Time's up.*

At the window, she leaned over. Townsfolk stood shouting at the walls of the tavern down below, holding pitchforks and torches. There was no escaping that way, and she turned to face the door, the only place she had left to go. Another door down the hall was thrown open, followed by another scream. This room was next, so Torenia did what she had grown up doing—hiding in the closet.

Dust and something earthy filled her nostrils. She held her breath as the door opened, hoping that the closet was not an obvious space to look. Familiar, heavy footsteps came into the room; her father. The sound of rustling reached her ears, but her pulse echoed in her head. Suddenly, the window slammed shut.

"Come out, Torenia. I know you're in here somewhere," her father taunted.

As silently as she could, Torenia went through the bag and pulled out one of the potions. It was too dark to see the color or if it even had a label. She had no idea what it did, but she had to take a chance. Poised to pounce, she waited until her father figured out where she was and yanked open the closet doors. She threw the contents of the phial at him. He screamed as he recoiled from her, the potion burning his skin, and Torenia dashed out the door of the room, down the stairs as fast as she could, and out through the back of the tavern.

The cold hit her. She breathed it in, hurting her lungs. She ran as fast as her feet would allow, slipping twice and landing hard in the snow. The smell of burning flesh was replaced with burning wood; the screams of Scarlett's birds broke Torenia's heart. Since they could not apprehend her, they took it out on what Scarlett had left behind, hurting the innocent women of the brothel, her beloved birds.

By the time Torenia reached the next house, she was filled with the need for revenge. Breaking into the unguarded stable, she approached a large black horse who nickered softly. He was at ease with her immediately; she guided him out of the stables and mounted him. Rahella flew overhead, watching the spectacle from above.

Atop her mount, Torenia glanced back over her shoulder. The tavern burned, a funeral pyre for all she had loved. The cheers of the people scared her; she dug her heels into the horse's flanks so that he would gallop. He would take her far away from this place, from this horrible town. But she made herself a promise—she would return with a vengeance one day to bring back what they had dealt her.

11

THE YEAR OF INDULGENCE

OSLEKA

Three Years Later

Torenia brought her lips to Nadia's neck, smelling the sweetness of roses and cinnamon on her skin. The wooden door they were pressed against creaked gently, but the noise of the busy tavern below drowned out the sound. Her hands slid underneath Nadia's skirt, her thoughts on the woman who had brought her warm drinks in the morning, casting soft, hungry looks at her each time they passed one another in the hallways.

The smoothness of Nadia's skin under Torenia's palm made her stomach twist as her fingers moved with ease and expertise. Women were so much more pleasant than men; there was a familiarity that Torenia lusted for. Men were too easy—all she had to do was cast a look and remove her clothes. With women, it was a dance, a passion one had to ignite.

Nadia's breath shook, louder and deeper, with each smooth movement of Torenia's trained hand. When her breath hitched, and her head tilted back against the door, Torenia kissed her neck again, unceasing until the moan filled the spaces between them. She stayed pressed against her, skirts bunched around their waists until Nadia could breathe again.

"Torenia..." Nadia said.

"Shh." She pressed her finger to Nadia's lips. "Don't make this more than it is. You know I'm only passing through."

Nadia nodded. "Can I at least give you—"

"Another night," Torenia said. "I have but one request."

A memory of being tucked away in a closet, wondering if she was beautiful or if she was the monster Aster and their mother said she was.

Nadia looked up at Torenia in the darkness of the storage closet. "Anything."

"Tell me I'm beautiful." The moment the words were out, Torenia wished she could take them back. Pitiful—this fear of not being what others desired crept up on her when she was in dark rooms, seeking praise.

"Torenia," Nadia said, her voice sultry, "you're the most beautiful woman I've ever met."

"Good night, Nadia," Torenia said, leaving the closet with a smile on her lips.

Her small room above the tavern was cozy, kept out the brutal Oslekan cold. Though she had no fireplace, the massive hearth downstairs kept the upper rooms comfortable. Torenia knelt on the floor, her dress splayed around her, measuring out an array of herbs and tinctures. Placing a cork in the small phial, she gave it a quick shake. The coin in the inner pocket of her skirts rattled about, reminding her just how little she had left. Her dreams of becoming a powerful witch had once fueled her; now, they were nothing more than bitter memories. This world did not favor women or witches, and she moved from place to place, never sticking around long enough to plant her roots and call one location home.

Success did not come as she had hoped when she was a naïve seventeen-year-old. Her dreams had withered as they would have had she remained in Silvania. Living on the run humbled her but also made her bitter. Her long, black hair hung over her shoulder.

She caught her reflection in the dark window but cast her eyes away —the woman she once imagined she saw in the mirror all those years ago was nothing more than a childish dream now.

The harsh life she lived was beginning to show. Though still youthful, she had dark circles beneath her eyes, making them appear sunken. Her skin was still tight and smooth, but she knew wrinkles would appear, first by her eyes, then her lips. The thought of losing her beauty, the very thing that gave her power, terrified her.

Despite everything Torenia had to sell to keep herself fed these past few years, she'd kept the little handheld mirror she had taken when she fled Silvania. Though she didn't stare into it while hidden away in closets anymore, she couldn't bear to part with it. Hardly a sentimental person, she wondered if she kept it as a reminder of those who had wronged her—Mother, Father, Aster, Adam.

Taking the cork out of the phial, Torenia drank back the tonic. Tension in her shoulders released, calmness spreading over her entire body. The cold nights when she was short on money were the hardest, the nights when she needed something extra to make it through. Shedding the stress like a snake does its skin, Torenia got to her feet. If she wanted a roof over her head tomorrow night, she needed to work for it. Counting the last of her coin, she sighed, then headed down to the tavern where she hoped someone would require her services.

Familiar noises of stools shuffling against uneven wooden floors, the crackle of the fire in the hearth, and mugs of ale clattering against each other soothed Torenia. She felt safe among the chaos, blending into the noise. She brought a small glass of vodka to her lips; the liquid burned her tongue, warming the pit of her stomach.

At the front of the bar, the door swung open, snow blowing in as if wanting to join the merriment of the tavern. No one glanced over when someone entered; it was busy and too late at night. Every patron was drunk, laughter and singing filling the air.

Torenia knew she had to move soon, not because she was low on funds, but because this town had welcomed her. She thought of Nadia and knew she was growing too comfortable. Tonight, this worked in her favor; whispers of who she was and what she was capable of had spread.

A hooded woman sat before her, appearing like a flash in Torenia's sight. She focused on her features, noting the black circles under her eyes that were not from lack of sleep. A cut crept up her cheek like a knife-caused smile. Gruesome, but nothing new to her.

"You're the traveling witch," the young woman said in a shaky voice. She knew her sobriquet, the title she had adopted. She reached out her gloved hands and grasped Torenia's.

Studying her, Torenia pinned her age at no more than eighteen years. Clearly terrified of even being there, she shook like a leaf. Having seen this time and time again, Torenia knew what she needed.

"Where can I find him?" Torenia whispered.

"No." The woman shook her head, and Torenia stiffened. "Do not harm him. I just...no longer wish to carry his child."

"No crime may go unpunished," Torenia said as she pulled her hands from the woman's, then reached over and removed the hood she wore. There were new and old bruises. "I can terminate the pregnancy for a small price. As for him, I will do what is necessary free of cost."

The woman pondered this, tears welling up in her brown eyes. The flesh around them was puffy and swollen. At the back of the bar, a pair of men had slung their arms around each other, swaying and singing abrasively. The noise was a good cover, for no one noticed the oddity of the only two women in the bar whispering to one another. Torenia learned that it was easier to hide in plain sight if she truly wished to remain invisible. She did not, however, want to be invisible forever.

"What would you do?" she asked.

Torenia leaned over and brushed the hair covering the woman's bruised face. "That depends. Who is he to you?"

"My husband," she whispered. "My parents couldn't afford to keep me any longer. I was a burden to them, so they married me off."

Torenia's lip curled into a scowl. "You rely on him for a house, for survival?"

The timid lady nodded. With her fists clenched atop her skirt, Torenia wished she could change the world, fix it for every woman who went through the same thing. The rape and the abuse, the blame and the desperation for survival. But she could only change the world one person at a time. It was not enough.

"What is your name?" she asked.

"Rada," the woman replied. Her eyes went wide with instant regret, fearing that she had exposed too much of herself to a stranger.

"Your name is safe with me," Torenia said to ease her worry. She felt the hair on her neck prickling, and she cast her attention to the corner of the bar. A man sat there, staring at her, through her. His slender figure was intimidating, even without the accompanying cold stare. This location was no longer safe, she decided.

She grabbed Rada's hand. "Your husband, is he out of the house?"

Rada shook her head. "Sleeping."

"Bring me there."

Torenia dressed and they slipped out into the harsh winter cold, the snow blasting them relentlessly. Even with the doors to the bar shut and the snow hiding them from prying eyes, she still felt his stare upon her back. A shudder rippled down her spine as she followed Rada with haste. The snow slowed them, but Torenia felt her shoulders relax after some time.

The house was in sight, no light coming from the windows, only a lantern on the porch to guide them. Rada opened the door and hurried Torenia inside. Hushed, walking with soft feet, they gathered in the modest living room, where a fire burned, low and dwindling. Rada placed a log upon the flames, watching the fire grow with a tender look on her face. Rage flickered across her features, and Torenia knew she was considering the second option—to kill her husband.

12

Walking through the small house, Torenia studied its emptiness. There was nothing personal about the home except for a discarded pipe and an open bottle of spirits sitting on the table. She ran her bare hand over the ledge, soot and dust staining her fingertips. Examining them, she wiped them on her skirt and faced Rada; it was time to get to business before the man inside the bedroom woke up and realized someone was in his home.

"We will not be able to undo this," she warned.

Rada nodded, clutching her hands together, nails digging into her skin.

Torenia turned and looked out of the window into the darkness. The fire reflected within the glass beside her own image. In the past few years, she had aged, but not poorly. Instead, she grew into her frame, filling it out in ways she could not as a youth. Her cheeks thinned in the years that she had gone hungry, the bones of her face jutting out just slightly. Though it made her look beautifully harsh, she felt the world had shaped her in its image, as the world was harsh.

Her hand deftly found a fold in her skirt where a small satchel hid. As she detached it, she turned to face Rada again. The young girl, too young to be pregnant, looked ashamed of her decision.

Torenia handed the small package full of baneful herbs and berries to Rada. "Mix this with milk and drink all of it," she explained. "It will stop the pregnancy."

Rada clutched the leather satchel like her life depended on it. She nodded gratefully, though terror remained in her eyes.

"Does he know?" Torenia asked, eyes on the girl's flat stomach.

She shook her head. "I have only missed one blood, but I am sure."

Torenia eyed the bedroom door, wanting to stride in and slit the man's throat while he slept. Part of the reason she was still alive today was in her title, the name circling: The Traveling Witch. She was always on the run and left very little evidence of her existence when she moved on.

She fished out another item, a handful of seeds, looking at Rada. "These are white cotton seeds. Use a mortar and pestle to crush them into a drink every day. For the rest of your time with him, he must drink this. It will cause infertility. Plant these seeds, make sure they grow, and harvest enough to get through the long winters here. It will be difficult, and you may fail. If you succeed, he will grow increasingly unhappy; he will begin to blame you. I can promise you that."

"But it would be his infertility, not mine..." Rada replied weakly.

"Men will never admit the trouble lies with them." If she had been a different sort of woman, Torenia would have held Rada's hands and tried to convince her of other options. She dealt with what she was asked, and she was always honest. "It will always be you who is defective."

Torenia had seen it over and over again. Her teas and potions could help with fertility, as she had done many times, but nothing she could do with seeds and plants could stop someone like Rada's husband. It took a knife or poison. They called her a witch, but much of what she did use was from the land around her, the very offerings of nature.

Rada removed a bracelet that she had been wearing underneath her jacket sleeve. It was quite large, made of pure silver. "It was my grandmother's," she explained, handing it to Torenia.

Torenia had been paid in many ways in the past, so sentimentality meant nothing to her. She gripped the bracelet, holding it up to let it glimmer in the moonlight while she studied it. This would bring in enough money to move her to another town, enough to keep her belly full for a few weeks. Tucking it into the pockets sewn within her skirts, she nodded curtly at Rada.

She watched as the young girl's lip quivered. Perhaps it was the last thing she had to remind her of someone who loved her. Maybe it was the last thing that she had of her family. None of this tugged on Torenia's heartstrings, but she reflected for a moment.

"I've given you more than you asked," Torenia told her. "A girl needs to eat."

"Y-yes," Rada stammered, "of course."

Torenia started for the door, pausing with her hand on the knob. Glancing over her shoulder, she queried, "Why will you not kill him?"

"You say that like it is easy." Rada's whisper came out harsh, accusatory.

"In time, you may understand. When he has waited years for you to bear children, he will eventually turn on you. Trust me, Rada, it will be easy for him." She had no more parting words for her. Some took her advice, some understood her words more than others. Some had to walk that path to understand.

Torenia was turning to the door when she heard a shuffling from behind that was not Rada. In the split second that followed, she had a decision to make: flee now, leaving Rada to face the wrath of her husband, or defend her. Rada's pleas to the man sauntering into the room were frantic. Reaching into the sleeve of her coat, she pulled out a blade and stepped between the terrified young woman and her husband.

"Who is this, Rada?" he shouted. "Tell me!"

"I-I do not know!" Rada lied through her tears.

His eyes narrowed into slits as he surveyed the situation. A stranger in his home, wielding a knife and blocking him from his wife. Torenia could see his mind piecing it together, trying to figure out who she was to his wife. A friend, a lover, or a witch?

"You will not touch her," Torenia spat.

His lip twitched in rage, warning her that he was going to attack. She had no choice but to defend herself, no matter what Rada wanted. She was seasoned in survival and, instead of backing down like he expected, she waited until he lunged for her and plunged the blade into his belly. Her spare hand gripped his shoulder to hold him there as he cried out, the cut not fatal yet.

"Rada," Torenia said, "the choice is yours."

Rada did not hesitate. "Do it."

She dragged the blade from right to left, slicing his belly open. Blood gushed over her, hot and thick. Stepping back, Torenia released the man. He fell to the floor, the blade with him. He bled out, his moans dying out like the pale light of a setting sun.

Rada dropped to her knees. "What have I done..."

Torenia's face remained stoic as she hoisted her back up. "Get on your feet, we will stage this as a break-in, a robbery. You will be looked after if that is what the town believes. But I need you to change into your bedclothes and follow my instructions. Do you understand?"

Rada nodded frantically.

While Rada changed, Torenia picked up her knife and wiped it clean on the back of her skirt. Placing it on the table, she stripped out of her bloody attire before throwing it into the fire. Entering the bedroom, she saw Rada shaking like a leaf. Ignoring the girl, she grabbed the dress she had been wearing and slipped into it, then approached Rada again, where she sat limply on the bed.

Torenia handed her back the bracelet. "Keep this. I'll take some valuables, as I see fit, for payment so the story of a robbery will be believable. After I have left and the snow has covered my tracks, run to the neighbors and tell them that a thief entered the house, but your husband woke up and confronted him. He was attacked and killed but fought valiantly to protect you."

Rada nodded.

"What did the man look like?" Torenia prompted.

Rada opened and closed her mouth like a fish. Torenia was about to slap the wits back into her when she finally answered. "Dark hair, but I couldn't see his face because there was no light. He was tall...b-burly."

"Keep it at that, nothing more," Torenia said firmly.

Rada nodded, then pulled out the satchel Torenia had given her. It was clear she now wished to have the child. Torenia said nothing, taking the satchel back. A pregnant widow would garner more sympathy.

Torenia left to find a few things to take with her. She found some coin and a necklace, stopping to remove a ring and pocket watch from the corpse. Stepping back into the cold, she felt a breeze against the wetness at the corner of her mouth. She wiped the back of her hand over it, a smudge of red staining her porcelain skin.

13

The inn shone like a beacon in the dark. Torenia quickened her pace, feeling the scratchy fabric of the rag-like dress chafing against her skin. Warmth practically radiated off the inn; she wished she could spend one more night there. The wind died down as she reached the wraparound porch. The building was faded, falling apart, but the rooms inside were clean. Lifting her skirt as she reached the bottom stair, she took them two at a time for efficiency, stomping her feet at the front door.

To shake off the murder on her hands.

"Late night for a pretty lady." The voice sent chills down her spine.

Glancing over at a swinging porch chair that would hold two, Torenia saw a man—the same one who had been staring at her in the bar earlier. Anxiety swept over her, but she stealthily touched her fingertips to the knife that sat snug in her sleeve. It had recently seen blood and perhaps would again tonight. Clutching the hilt, she made no further action to encourage or to insult him. All she had to do was open the door and disappear into the safety of her room. She only needed a few minutes to pack.

"I had business to attend to."

"Must have been urgent, it's a blizzard out here."

"The weather is never something to shy away from." She believed this wholeheartedly, embracing each season; everything the earth gave her was power. The seasons brought death, and death brought life.

"What sort of business was so important that you risked frost*bite*?" He accented the word 'bite.'

Torenia dipped her head, wanting to duck inside but not daring to turn her back on this strange man. All she needed were her bags and her horse, then she could disappear to the next town. The soft clack of her raven's talons on the porch railing helped her relax; Rahella was a fierce friend and protector.

"I am a midwife," Torenia said. "But a lady's business is not yours, so I will speak no more on the matter. Good night to you, sir."

He rose from the chair, the lantern that hung outside the front door making his skin glow orange. She thought bitterly of her father. When he drew closer, blocking the doorway with his large frame, Torenia could smell the stench of alcohol on his breath. There was enough for her to detect it, but not enough to make his movements sloppy.

Palming her knife, she knew she had to make her move soon. His head was high, throat exposed, but he was not so tall that she couldn't deliver a fatal swipe with her weapon. Before she had the chance, another man stepped onto the porch. Torenia feared the worst; she could feel his presence as he climbed up the stairs, which groaned under his weight. Behind them, Rahella quorked.

"Vlad, you will not harm this woman," he said. His voice was not deep, but his tone commanded respect.

Vlad looked Torenia up and down, then nodded to show his obedience to the other man. He pulled off his fur hat and ran his fingers through his thinning hair, casting one last glance at Torenia before maneuvering out of her way. Within seconds, he had walked down the stairs and disappeared into the flurry of snow.

Alone with the second man, Torenia kept her knife in hand and turned to face him. Shadows warped his face; Torenia shifted so the single lantern could shed more light upon him. Bright blue eyes pierced through her; the man wore no smile as he waited patiently for Torenia to do or say something. His long, black coat billowed in the wind, his gloved hands positioned in front of his stomach. His slicked-back blonde hair, shaved at the sides, made him look younger than he was and revealed the tattoos coming up from his back and around his neck.

"You can put the knife away," he said. "I mean you no harm."

"That is something I've heard too frequently before someone attempts to harm me," Torenia said, hand still on the hilt. Sweat coated her palms despite the cold.

"My name is Roman Sokolov." He extended his hand.

She hesitated to shake it, but something about him compelled her to hear what he had to say. She reached out and took his hand, feeling the warmth radiating from it. She longed to be indoors where she wouldn't be shivering from the cold. This place was unforgiving; the weather had no concerns about how well any living creature might fare. It killed the weak, leaving only the strong. The survivors —something Torenia always considered herself to be.

Moving swiftly, Roman walked towards the door and gestured for her to enter. She turned to watch him join her in the foyer, unwilling to let him sneak up on her again.

"That man outside, you knew him?" she asked. "How can I be sure that your intentions are any different from his?"

"I doubt you have an inkling of what his intentions were," Roman said. He headed up the stairs, clearly expecting her to follow.

"Enlighten me," Torenia demanded.

Roman looked towards the hall of rooms and, without a word, headed towards hers. She cursed herself for not having a contingency plan. She'd grown too comfortable.

Standing just outside of the room, he waited for her to open the door. She felt drawn to him; he had a charm that was inviting, even enticing. He felt like the embodiment of power, something Torenia wanted.

"I see so much potential in you," he said at last. "I have been seeking you for some time now."

It was not often that men came to her for her abilities, and she was always skeptical about them. Roman, in particular, did not look like a man who lacked anything. Perhaps on the outside, he gave off the impression that he had everything he ever wanted but suffered for something else internally. Impotence was a common issue Torenia helped with, but she suspected it was not the reason he had sought her out. She could not pin him down, but she wanted to. She needed to.

She looked him dead in the eye, refusing to show fear, then unlocked the door to her room. A cold gust of air came from the open window, and Rahella perched on the sill, watching them with dark eyes. They glistened in the lantern light, Roman watching the large raven with fascination.

"My services come at a cost," she said, though she still suspected he had not come for herbs and tonics. He said he saw potential in her, but for what, she wondered.

"I do not need what you can offer me. I am offering you what you need," he said, as he reached into his coat and pulled out a flask, raising it to his lips.

When he lowered it again, Torenia thought she saw red on his lips, but he wiped it away too quickly. Red wine, she told herself.

"What is it that I need?" She herself wasn't sure of the answer anymore. The dreams of a little girl, once hidden away in a closet, had faded long ago.

"Eternal beauty and power."

It was as if he knew her deepest secrets, her childish dreams.

14

I t had been years since Torenia looked in the mirror and asked if
she was the fairest of them all. When she left behind Silvania, she
left behind those childish notions. But they always lingered, hidden
somewhere deep inside her. With all the people in the world, she
knew she would never be the most beautiful. But eternal beauty—
that was something she never before considered. Once the seed was
planted in her mind, she knew she needed it.

But she could not show Roman her desperation.

Instead, she walked toward the window where Rahella perched.
Stroking the raven's head, she felt her slick feathers, soft and smooth
like silk. The animal was more than a simple raven; she was a part of
Torenia herself. No other living creature ever shared a stronger
connection than a witch and her familiar. Bound eternally until
death...but what if death never came?

"I would like to know your intentions. Lay them out clearly for
me." She knew that Roman wanted her to join him; she held the
power in her hands. What did he want from her? What did he think
he would gain if she joined him? Why was he offering her exactly
what she had always wanted, down to her core?

"As I have said, I see potential in you. One I do not think you see."
Roman remained stock still.

"Say you really are able to give me eternal beauty and power, what purpose does it serve you?" Torenia grabbed a decanter and poured herself a glass of whisky. "Would you like a glass?"

"I have my own," he replied, "thank you."

She capped the decanter and swirled the dark honey liquid inside the glass. Sipping it, she looked up at him and waited for more answers.

"You are famous in more than one city, more than one country, even. One may argue you are more notorious than your ancestor, Azalea."

Torenia repressed a smile. Flattery would not win her over, but it still brought forth pride. She wondered how much he knew about her family. She had not given her true name, but he knew so much about her. It unnerved her.

"With fame comes risk. I know this far too well," he continued.

"I have never heard your name before; perhaps you are not as famous as you think." Torenia knew better than to taunt, but couldn't help herself.

Roman laughed, and Torenia thought she noticed something peculiar about him. There was something strange about him from the moment she had first met him but she could not quite put her finger on it. In that flash of laughter, she thought she saw elongated teeth. Her mind spun; the tattoos, the pointed teeth, was he a part of some cult? She'd heard whispers before of cults of werewolves and other, more dangerous creatures.

"No, I do not believe you would have ever heard of me," Roman said. "I am a part of the Brotherhood; perhaps you have heard that name?"

"Once or twice," she admitted. "A blood cult?"

His eyebrows raised. "It could be called that, perhaps."

"If you do not wish to tell me everything, I will not take your empty promises and gifts. I refuse to be indebted to a man whom I cannot trust, and I have never known a man I could trust." She gestured toward the door. "Tell me or leave."

"How about I show you?" he suggested, his tone becoming something darker, more serious. Although his demeanor went from light to somewhat threatening, she felt a tug at that moment. Torenia sensed a darkness in Roman that matched her own.

Holding the door for her like a gentleman, he followed her out of the room, then walked ahead of her to the end of the hall.

A faint coughing came through the walls, a shudder running through Torenia. She did not know what to expect from this. With long, slender fingers, he opened the unlocked door to reveal a sickly man lying in a bed, his arm extended, a bloodied handkerchief in his weak hand.

Finger by finger, he removed his gloves, revealing grotesquely long nails, blackened with grime underneath. Tucking the gloves into his pocket, he walked over to the man. Roman placed his hand against the man's head, pushing him back against the sweat-stained pillow. Torenia watched in pure fascination as he leaned down to the man's exposed throat, the throbbing in her ears making all the other noises fade. A gargled scream shattered the bubble of silence, and she covered her mouth as she witnessed something grotesque and beautiful all at once.

Moments slipped by as Roman feasted. His nails had plunged into the man's throat along with his teeth; he withdrew them slowly, blood dripping to the floor, as he wiped the stains of red from his mouth with the back of his hand.

"This," his voice hoarse at first, then smooth again like velvet, "is the cost."

Torenia had heard legends of many creatures when she was a child; the stories of werewolves were deeply ingrained in who she was. Though she didn't believe that the Wolf of Silvania really preyed on young girls, she knew now of other dangerous things. Witches had always existed, according to the stories her mother told, and they became real when she realized how much knowledge they had. When Scarlett Răceanu had taken her in and taught her the craft, she knew more creatures had to be out there.

But she had never faced a nightwalker before.

Roman stepped up to her as he replaced his gloves, placing a hand on her cheek. Eternal beauty hung just within her reach, but she did not know if she had the stomach to do what needed to be done. A battle had raged inside of her for so long, a battle against the darkness she was born with. Where had that gotten her? It was time to embrace the Luca within her.

"I…" Her words failed her.

"I have seen what you are capable of, my dear," he whispered, the bounce in his voice returning. "I know that you are strong enough."

He was right. She wondered if, somehow, Roman had seen what she did to Rada's husband.

Power and beauty—she wanted it so badly. The desire sank deep into her core, starting in the pit of her stomach and weaving through her veins into her heart. With each pulse of blood, she felt desire wrap its fingers around her, gripping each part of her. This stranger, who had opened himself up in front of her, dangled her desire right in front of her. His thumb smoothly rubbed her pale cheek.

"What would you sacrifice for power? For beauty?" He taunted, whispering in her ear so softly that his words were barely gusts of wind against her flesh. "For eternity?"

"Everything," she replied. "Anyone."

15

"Will it hurt?" Torenia asked, taking a seat on the edge of the bed. They had returned to her room, and she thought about how easily Roman had left the body behind, as though he had no fear of the ramifications that could come from it. Did he have so much power that he could leave bodies in his wake? Or did he not care about being caught because he was a vampire?

Roman placed his hand on her cheek again. "Yes."

She appreciated his honesty. Glancing at her agitated familiar in the window, she shook her head to calm the raven. A familiar's job was to help teach, protect, and guide young witches. Torenia was no longer a young witch, and she no longer needed protection. She brought her feet up and leaned back against the hay-filled mattress.

"After it is over, where will we go?" she asked Roman. Her blue eyes matched his; it was like looking in a mirror.

"The Brotherhood," he told her. "A place of acceptance for people like us."

"But I am not like you," she said. "The world is cruel to women, and the 'brotherhood' doesn't sound like a place where a woman would be welcomed."

"You aren't like me yet," he replied, "and they will welcome you because it is my will." He closed her eyes with his fingers. The slight pressure of his fingertips on her eyelids was strange; uncomfortable, but somehow, comforting. She was surprised that her breathing remained steady. When she felt his breath upon her neck and tensed; his hand touched her cheek gently, and the tightness eased. How could a man—a vampire—have such a soft touch?

Even as Roman sunk his teeth into her throat, the pain blinding her, she knew he had been gentle. He groaned slightly, forcing himself to stop, and threw his head back. She realized he had fed before in order to control himself so he could stop before he killed her. He removed a white handkerchief from his jacket pocket and pressed it against the wound, the pain in her neck subsiding to a dull throb.

"Is that al—" She shrieked in pain before she could finish the sentence. It raced through her bloodstream like a parasite with every throb of the wound. Thick black lines, like those from blood poisoning, wound up her neck and over her chest towards her heart. She writhed in pain as Roman watched from where he sat beside her. Gently, he patted her shoulder twice.

"It will be over soon," he told her, rising from the bed and casually striding over to the window. Rahella quorked, her feathers ruffling. When Roman neared, she flashed her razor-sharp talons. With a jerky movement, he forced Rahella to back out of the window, slamming it shut, then closed the curtains and blew out the lantern, darkness enveloping the room. Overseeing her agony, he stood at the foot of the bed, a smile playing on his lips.

The pain worsened, worse than anything Torenia had ever felt in her life. Her back arched off of the bed, shoulders digging into the mattress. Her heart hammered, pounding so hard she thought it would burst. Roman's presence was no longer comforting; he did not care how much pain she was in or how terrified she was. He simply watched her transformation with fascination.

Hours felt like days as time passed; the pain never ebbed, only worsened. She felt the change deep inside of her, consuming every part of her that once was. Her humanity disappeared, the darkness warping and twisting her. Her nails dug deep into her palms, slicing the calloused flesh. Just when she thought the pain would finally consume her, it faded as though it never existed.

Her eyes jerked open, bringing more pain than she could have experienced in a lifetime in a single moment. Tears slid down her cheeks, getting lost in her hair. Eventually, the only pain she felt was a light throb in her palms.

When she felt steady, she swung her legs off the side of the bed and planted her feet on the ground. She marveled at her hands and the fact that she could see them so well in the dark. Cocking her head to the side, she glanced at Roman with questions in her eyes. The scent of her own blood overwhelmed her; she could not stop herself from salivating.

Striding over to her side, he took out his flask and brought it to her lips. She pushed it away, turning her head, but the scent caught her attention. Gingerly, she glanced back at it, then allowed Roman to tilt it, the blood inside warm from being pressed against his body. The taste was overwhelming, something that she had never experienced before. No matter how hungry she had been in her life, nothing had ever satisfied her like the blood did at that moment. Her hands reached up to take the flask, and she finished off what was inside of it.

Blood dribbled from the corner of her mouth when it was empty. Roman ran his thumb over the droplet, smearing it across her lower lip, as she caught a glimpse of herself in the window. With her stunning blue eyes and pale skin, the red streak stood out, making her look even more wicked.

Roman pocketed the empty flask and took her hands in his own, gripping them firmly. He knew the words that she wanted to hear, and he leaned towards her ear to whisper them like a secret.

"You will look beautiful upon a throne." His voice caressed her inner desire.

16

Cloaked in her warmest clothing, Torenia hoisted herself up onto her horse—the same one she had stolen so many years ago. She could feel the blood pulsing through the old beast beneath her as she stroked his muscular neck. The horse nickered nervously, sensing the change in his rider. Rahella swooped down from the building, and Torenia noted that her movements were angry. She raised her arm that bore a protective brace, but the bird landed on her shoulder, digging her talons deeper than necessary. She shrugged off the familiar. "You can fly the whole way, then."

Rahella made no noise but soared high enough that Torenia lost sight of the raven. Her familiar would adjust, but she made no attempt to understand whatever was bothering the bird. A younger Torenia would have followed Roman with more caution, but she was tired of running, of living a life where she had to fight for every meal. Couldn't Rahella understand that?

Beside her, on another mount, was Roman. He guided his horse to turn around, and they began their journey.

"How many days of travel will it be?" Torenia asked when they had reached a comfortable pace. The muscular horse beneath her walked effortlessly. She was grateful for her enhanced sight in the dark, but it would have been tedious, at best, to go by foot.

"Not far," he said, still looking ahead at the path. "We will need to stop before daybreak to feed and rest. I will teach you how to hunt then, how to be lethal."

"Do you worry about people discovering you?" she asked.

"There are so many creatures in this world other than man. Man fears all that is not the same as he is; you should know that, Torenia." He glanced at her. "Would you like to know why I chose you?"

"My potential?" She blurted out, the words half-mockery. She knew there was more to his reasons, and what he wasn't disclosing intrigued her.

"You see the world as it is. You understand the evil man can do; you've seen it."

"How is it you know what I have seen?"

"The Luca name is known across the continent. I learned of the legend through stories and books. When I obtained my position, I discovered many written works about your ancestors. I must admit, I was curious about the Wolf that your family controls, but it was a witch I sought. The stories led my scouts to your home. They reported back, and I learned of your daring escape. Your ambition intrigued me."

"I am not my ancestor. I scarcely believe there is a Wolf. If there is, he's been turned into lore to keep girls scared and obedient."

"Your family carries great power. Not the Wolf—powerful as he is, he can only be used for one bloodline, with each daughter sacrificed. Powerful in a small village such as your own, less so when you begin to think bigger. No, Torenia, your power is within your ruthless Luca blood."

Torenia thought of her sister learning scraps of witchcraft through a book passed down for centuries to each new generation of Lucas.

"Aster..." Torenia mumbled, wondering how recently Roman had been to Silvania. It frightened her to think of how long he had been searching for her. "Did your scouts see my family?"

"My dear, they are not your family. Not really." His voice hitched, playful, yet also taunting.

She knew it was true, so she held her tongue. Despite wanting to know what had become of her family, she refused to beg him for information.

She sensed that his next words were chosen carefully. "Family is not always blood. Blood can walk away without looking back." He spat the words like venom now. "And take with him so much more than he knows."

"You lost someone?"

"We were three brothers from humble beginnings—not unlike your own, another reason I chose you. We rose to power to fight for the nightwalkers of the country. You, my dear, are a half-blooded vampire, created rather than born. The Pure Bloods may look down on you and wish to rid the world of you. We fought for equality among vampires."

"You need a Half Blood on the throne?" she inquired.

"No, my dear, I am a Half Blood. My brother Ivan is a Half Blood. Our youngest brother, Nikolai, is Pure Blooded. He was a natural-born vampire, whereas Ivan and I were turned. He walked away from the power, from the throne—the very one I am offering you. I need someone with more power than a vampire, someone like you. You have the potential to be so much more than a traveling witch who terminates pregnancies and poisons abusive husbands. You will never make a dent in these evils, but beside me, you can help keep balance."

Torenia grimaced at his words; she knew she could be more but did not know how. Without Scarlett, she could only learn so much through books and trial and error. Living on the run would always prevent her from having true power. Perhaps, without fear of being caught and murdered, with someone like Roman behind her, she would reach higher places—be the strongest of them all. She grinned at him, her newly sharpened teeth flashing.

They traveled many nights together, finding food and shelter along the way. As they drew closer to where Roman and Ivan lived, the innkeepers began to recognize him. It was with great fear that they offered Roman free lodging, though he still paid them handsomely.

"Things will get easier," Roman told Torenia in her room. She always had her own. "I have a supply."

It made Torenia uncomfortable to think about what a supply of blood entailed, but she carefully hid her discomfort from him.

"Before I allow you into my home, you must be able to do this." Roman held the flask out of her reach; she had been drinking from it instead of killing, but she was ready now. She had been ready the moment she woke up a nightwalker, but Roman was doing this to prove he had control over her. He hadn't let her feed, stating she wasn't ready yet.

"I am a Luca, as you have so frequently reminded me." She didn't reach for the flask. "I am ready."

Standing in the room together, she waited as still as a statue as he grabbed her chin. His gloved hand held her gently—it was more unsettling than if he had been firm—as he leaned in. "My brother will kill you if you cannot do this. He does nothing without my consent, but if you fail—"

"I understand that," she said, pulling away from his grasp. "As I said, I am ready."

He softened just enough for Torenia to notice the change. Clasping his hands in front of him, he dipped his head and spoke. "Come. The woman you will meet tonight may look innocent. However, the innkeeper informed me that she sells children on the black market."

Torenia curled her lip in disgust. "Then you make it too easy."

He grinned in response and opened the door to the hall. Torenia exited after him, and the wooden hallway floorboards groaned relentlessly, making stealth impossible. But Roman did not worry about such trivial things. Removing a glove when he reached their destination, he rapped his knuckles on the door three times. The sound was cheerful, a stark contrast to what waited outside the door.

The door cracked open, brown eyes peering out from the darkness of the room.

"Yes?" The woman asked.

Roman shoved forward, not caring to be gentle or use his words to trick this woman into letting them in. She staggered back as the door hit her, gasping as she fell to the ground with a loud thud. Torenia walked in, eyes on her victim the whole time, savoring the fear in her eyes. When she looked closer, she saw it.

The woman resembled Aster, or what she supposed Aster might look like in ten years.

"What do you want?" she cried, scrambling back against the bed. "I will yell for someone to come!"

"No one is coming for you," Roman said.

Torenia supposed she should feel bad, but she was unable to. This was a good start, she thought. She had to do this. She wondered briefly if, when Roman found her family, he had seen Aster and orchestrated this. How much of what he was telling her was true, and how much of it was carefully crafted lies?

"Are you alone, my dear?" he asked as he knelt down, his ungloved hand settling on her cheek.

The woman nodded, tears dribbling down her face. Her mouth was twisted from terror; she would have been beautiful if she wasn't sobbing. Even though Torenia thought she would have reacted similarly should their roles have been reversed, she thought the woman before her was utterly pathetic. Recalling what Roman had accused her of—selling children on the black market—disgust filled her. She didn't buy her tears for a second.

Roman rose and glanced at Torenia. Like a master would their dog, he nodded to her, a signal that she was free to do as she pleased. In that second, she hated him. He offered her power but treated her like she was beneath him. Perhaps one day, she would take his power from him. The thought made her step towards the woman. Do Roman's bidding now, and steal his power later.

Although she was hungry, hungrier than she realized, something held her back. Was Roman lying?

He sensed this and walked behind her, placing his hands on her shoulders as he whispered in her ear. His voice was like velvet, melodic and smooth. "Tell me, Torenia, who do you hate most in this world?"

"My sister." She did not need to think about the answer and knew why he had asked the question. He played mind games, always. She would have to proceed with utmost caution.

Stepping forward without any more guidance, she knelt down in front of the cowering woman. Her mind ran through every evil thing Aster had done to her and how she got away with all of it. Her mind went blank as she sensed the pulse of the woman's blood; she pushed the dense brown hair away from her throat, shoving her head back violently. Her scream was cut off by Torenia's swiftness; even her whimpers faded when she bit down into her throat.

It came to her naturally.

The pulse of the woman's blood through her veins was like nothing Torenia had ever felt before. Each heartbeat, rapid as it was, she felt through another person. The richness of such flavor, so different from the flask, it would never be matched. When she had consumed as much as she could, she threw her head back. Only then did she realize the woman's hands were now limp at her sides.

She rose from the corpse and took a deep, satisfied breath.

Behind her, Roman exhaled, satisfied. "I had my doubts about you, but Torenia, I think we are going to get along very well."

17

The building before Torenia was a castle; she had never seen one and certainly never imagined she would live in one. It perched atop a snowy hill, three stories tall with four towers, each of them embellished with pinnacles. The stone shone dull gray in the darkness of the night, but each window glowed with lamplight. Snow covered the pitched roofs; it looked like something out of a storybook. Hedges stretched from the sides, seeming to go on for miles. Amazed by its beauty, Torenia loosened her grip on the reins, letting her horse follow Roman on its own while she studied the ornate building.

As they neared the entrance, the castle seemed to loom even taller above them. The entrance was six meters tall, flanked by great white pillars holding up a balcony. There had been renovations done, that much was clear; ancient construction was married with newly built structure. Torenia tried to imagine what it had taken to fight for a place so well fortified. That was the kind of power she wanted.

A man clad in gray came to help Torenia off her horse, and she landed gracefully in the deep snow. Statues stood in the center of a large path leading to the castle entrance; they seemed human-esque based on their vague forms under the snow. Her bags were gathered by another man, and her horse was led away. Two men addressed Roman's needs, and she decided she could feel quite at home in a place like this. For years, she had been fending for herself; all that hard work while she was living on the run was finally paying off. She could get used to having someone at her beck and call.

"Where is Ivan?" Roman asked one of the staff.

"The back, *Korol*."

Roman nodded, reaching for Torenia's arm. The warm coat she wore was thick and padded, but she knew now that his touch was often gentle. With her free hand, she brushed snow from the fox pelt wrapped around her shoulders. He guided her along the path, diverting them down a smaller pathway that wound around the edges of the castle.

She wondered what the castle looked like in the other seasons. Did the snow ever go away in its entirety? She was suddenly ripped from her thoughts when she heard an animalistic roar, followed by a more human attempt at a response.

"What was what?"

"That," Roman said, a smile in his tone, "is Ivan."

They crested the hill the castle rested on, overlooking a series of dormant gardens. Up ahead, there was a glow from a dozen hanging lanterns, a façade of warmth. Another roar tore through the air, followed by maniacal laughter. Reaching the scene, Torenia watched in shock as she took in the sight before her.

A man, whom Torenia could only assume was Ivan, stood face to face with a large brown bear. Ivan circled, and the bear thrust its head back in anger, maw opening wide to show its killer teeth; they put the vampires' fangs to shame.

"Come on!" Ivan yelled, slapping his hands hard against his chest before spreading his massive arms wide.

The bear made a sort of bark in response and charged at Ivan. The broad beast of a man was prepared, placing one foot behind to steady his stance, then slipping out of the bear's path. He swung his arms around the animal's neck and clung tight. The bear attempted to shake him off but was unable. It began to chuff and bellow, trying to get onto its hind legs, before the bear stumbled, laying down.

From his position latched onto the suffocating bear, Ivan spotted Torenia, his crazed eyes glistening in the glow from the lanterns. His face broke into a grin, but the bear sensed his distraction and rolled onto Ivan, crushing him to the ground. He shouted curses from under the beast, tightening his arms around it again, but his momentary release gave the bear the air it needed. It rose up again, launching Ivan off its back.

Ivan rolled when he hit the ground, groaning loudly enough for Torenia to hear from a safe distance away. He got up slowly, in just enough time to see the bear coming for him again. He braced for impact as the animal reared onto its hind legs and swiped, clawing Ivan from chest to cheek. She smelled his blood from where she stood.

"Ivan," Roman called. "I think that is enough for tonight."

Ivan licked his lips, then whistled a quick two-tone melody.

The bear chuffed again, dropping to all fours, before proceeding to lie down.

"Good boy, Baltazar," Ivan said. He smeared the blood away from his face with the back of his forearm. "You'll be well-fed tonight."

Ivan gave the bear's fur a ruffle, then approached Roman and Torenia. His arms were wide, a big grin across his bloodied face. She watched as the two brothers embraced, a hand upon the back of the other's head, then a kiss on each cheek, before they parted.

"Welcome back, brother," Ivan exclaimed, clapping his hands together in excitement. He turned immediately to Torenia. "And what have you brought with you? Dinner? Ah—" He breathed in. "No, something far more exciting."

"Ivan, this is Torenia." Roman's voice was casual, but an underlying sense of caution lurked in his tone. "She is the witch I left to find. The Luca."

Torenia was flattered, but it withered when Ivan approached her. He stood only a few centimeters away from her, his breath smelling of spirits and blood. Under his penetrating gaze, she felt as though all her secrets were being revealed; she could not help the blush that crept across her cheeks.

Ivan was giddy, but he simply smiled. "Exquisite."

"You will speak to her and treat her as an equal, brother," Roman warned him.

"An equal," Ivan echoed. He brought his lips to her right cheek, then her left. When his lips brushed against her warm cheek, he whispered, "Or perhaps something more."

Torenia responded with a sharp intake of breath. He stepped back, but the grin never left his face, just as the hunger never left his eyes. She rubbed her arms and stepped back from Ivan. "After the long days—*nights* of travel, I wish for nothing more than a bath and a bed."

His grin somehow grew wider until Roman placed his strong hand on his shoulder. He reached his other hand out for Torenia to grab, his nails digging into his brother's muscle and bone. There was tension between them, and Torenia knew that, though Roman would look out for her, she had to look out for herself as well. He wanted her there, on that throne, to replace their youngest brother; he needed her but for his own means to an end.

"Go wash up, you're filthy," Roman told Ivan.

Ivan's eyes flashed with something that made her skin prickle.

Releasing his brother, Roman guided Torenia up the stairs and into the great enveloping warmth of the castle. She could still feel Ivan's icy cold eyes on her from a distance, his words rolling in the back of her mind as she entered the castle. She wasn't naïve enough to misunderstand Ivan's meaning; she would use it to her advantage.

Roman briefly explained the layout of the castle as they walked through, the entrance leading to a massive throne room. Inside, there were doors leading to all sorts of curious places, but they went straight to the stairs, lined with a crimson carpet. Paintings were staggered on the walls, images of decapitated beings and bodies slumped over each other, one showing a heap of corpses burning. Despite the disturbing content, Torenia could not look away. Somehow, she knew they were vampires.

Roman flagged down a servant dressed in gray. "Draw a bath for our Sister."

The woman bowed her head. "Yes, *Korol*."

"Tell me about *your* sister," Roman said.

"There is not much to say; she is wretched," Torenia admitted freely. "Her jealousy drove me out of my home. Many people died because of her, and I was almost one of them."

"If she saw you now, what would she say? What would she do?"

"She would ask you to do to her what you have done to me." Torenia knew Aster would want this life, a life of money and grandiosity, an exquisite lifestyle. "She would make you think she was better than me, prettier than me, more powerful than me. More *worthy* of all this."

"I would not believe her," Roman said as they continued their ascent.

"You say this now," Torenia mused.

"If I brought her here to you, threw her down at your feet while you sat upon a throne, would she beg for her life?" Roman's question reminded her of her own.

"I hope so." She glanced at him, a grin on her lips. "Tell me, Roman—do you have that kind of power?"

"Yes." He nodded, pushing open a door to reveal a beautiful bedroom. Tall ceilings and a large four-poster canopy bed caught her eye, and the sound of water being stirred with a hand beckoned her.

The young maid left the adjoining bathroom, curtsying again. The surge of power that swept through Torenia made her heart skip. She did not even realize that she had walked to the bathroom until she saw the large marble tub, steam billowing from it. She'd always had lukewarm baths in the inns and at her home many years ago.

She removed her cloak, dropping it to the ground. It puddled at her feet like a pool of black water, and she unlaced the bodice of her dress with deft fingers, letting it slip from her shoulders to join the pool of fabric at her feet. "I have a request," she said, turning to look over her shoulder, eyes on Roman.

Roman was unfazed by her blatant nudity. "I have no intention of making sexual advances toward you, Torenia. Do not think that is why I brought you here."

She laughed, quietly pleased that Roman felt this way, the power within her flourishing. "That was not my request."

He cocked his head slightly to the side, interested in what she had to say.

"There is a man I seek, Felix Răceanu." Until this moment, she had not known what her first move with this new power would be, yet deep down, she knew it was what she had to do to balance the scales and start abolishing her past.

"Very well."

Torenia knew Roman would not know why she wanted Felix and kept her reasons to herself. All she knew was that his intrigue and desire to impress and accommodate her would ensure that he brought this man to her. Her next words were spoken out of sheer curiosity.

"If you are not interested, perhaps you should send your brother in to see me," she said, stepping into the bathtub.

18

Torenia bathed every single night, a luxury she never thought she would be able to afford. Servants came at every ring of the bell, bringing her anything she wanted. She had been at the castle for a fortnight and already felt as though she was the queen she was meant to be. A special event was to take place that night; she forced herself to step out of the hot bath to get ready for the evening.

Drawing a white robe around her frame, she studied herself in the large mirror. Her figure was curvaceous with a leanness that came from her previous lifestyle, even with the steam distorting its reflection. Entering the bedroom, she noticed something on her bed. A large black box with a red bow beckoned her closer. As she lifted the box lid, she eyed the dress inside. It was black, almost entirely lace, the bodice lined with silk. Lifting it up to her body, she studied the cap sleeve gown; the low neckline and corset back would accentuate her figure exactly how she preferred. It was like nothing she had ever seen before; it was certainly not in style, but she never had fit into society's mold.

Before she began dressing for the evening, which Roman had kept a secret from her, there was a knock on the door. She assumed it would be a maid to help her tie the lacing of the corset so, tightening the belt of her robe, she told them to enter.

To her surprise, it was Ivan. His hair was slicked back, the tattoos creeping up from his back onto his neck, matching the ones on the side of his head. His tattoos matched his brother's, she noticed; she envied the solidarity of their relationship. She wondered if Nikolai had them too; if so, the ink did little to bind them.

"Good evening, Ivan," she said. "Your face healed up nicely."

"I like to keep my face pretty," he replied.

"I like a little...ruggedness," she said with a flirtatious tone.

Ivan grinned. "I can be rugged."

There was something ruthless about Ivan, something terrifying. It was in the way he obeyed Roman, yet still lingered on the edges, testing his brother's limits. Torenia knew that he could prove to be a powerful ally when she rose above Roman.

"You'll have to show me sometime," she said.

He flashed a grin, blue eyes matching hers.

"What can I help you with?" she asked, one hand on the bedpost, the other dangling at her side.

"A little bird told me that you had asked for me," he said.

The words ran through her mind, reminding her of Scarlett and her birds. Sadness swept over her, but she quickly locked it away, not daring to show Ivan that anything could bother her. To be a Sister in the Brotherhood would prove challenging; she could not let something from her past create any emotion in her. She, too, had to be ruthless.

She had to be wicked.

Roman offered her power, but she had to reach and take it for herself.

"Yes, I did." Torenia nodded in agreement, recalling that, on her arrival, she had requested that Roman send Ivan. He never did send Ivan that night, leaving her to her own devices, but the word had spread, just as she'd hoped. "I'm fascinated by you, by what you do. I want you to teach me, to show me everything about this world. I also heard that your library is rather extensive and, should I learn to be the most powerful witch, I must have access to all your reading material."

A flicker of disappointment flashed over his face but, just like

Torenia hid her sadness from him, he tucked it away. It was clear he had heard that her request for him had come when she was stark naked in the bath. Though she was hardly clothed now, she was not in the mood to flirt with danger. Not yet. Ivan had to be led along a little longer if she wanted her power over him to be sustainable.

She had an event to attend.

"Tomorrow, I will show you the library, and soon after, the harvest."

"I do have one more request." She smirked.

He waited, a menacing grin that would scare anyone away on his face. Anyone except Torenia. She'd seen a different kind of evil, and Ivan's sadistic fascination for bloodshed did not make him evil in her eyes.

She disrobed, then gestured to the dress. "Would you assist me?"

Instantly Ivan knew that this put him on a different level than Roman, which was her intent. If Roman found out what was going on, he would not respond well. He had his own way of seeing Torenia —as an equal who deserved Nikolai's spot on the throne. He sought to protect her. But Ivan would not turn down such an open request, and she knew it. When he met Torenia's stare, his eyes said everything—this must never reach Roman.

Ivan stood mere inches away as she stepped into the gown, sliding it up her body, then pressing her hands to her breasts, holding the dress tight. He began to lace the corseting in the back, his fingers more agile than she expected. He cinched it so tight that she gasped, feeling her ribs tighten and her stomach clench to make room. When he had finished lacing it, he draped her black hair over her shoulder, her shoulder blades jutting out from the top of the gown, as she felt his breath on her back.

"I have a gift for you," Ivan said, "from Roman."

She turned to face him, studying his crazed eyes. From his pocket, he removed a small tube. He spoke firmly, but not loudly. "Roman wishes you wear this."

She removed the cap from the tube, revealing a bright red lip stain. She licked her lips instinctively, remembering Scarlett. She always had red lips, and where she was from it was associated with the women in the brothel. Torenia raised a hand to her lips, touching them with her index and middle fingers.

"When does he expect me?" she asked.

"One hour," Ivan told her. "I'll send the maid in."

Moments after he left, a maid came in, shaking like a leaf. Torenia took the maid's delicate hand, looking at the beautiful girl. She did not recognize her.

"How old are you?" Torenia asked as she took a seat.

The maid stood behind her, brushing Torenia's hair with utmost care. Not a hair was pulled or tugged as her fingers began to braid. She answered in a meek whisper, "Sixteen, *Koroleva*."

"You are very beautiful." Torenia looked at her through the vanity mirror.

"Thank you," she said, averting her eyes and focusing on Torenia's hair.

"What is your name?"

"My name is Irina."

"How did you come to work here?" Torenia inquired.

The girl tensed and shook her head. "It is not important."

"I asked you a question; the importance of such is not your decision to make."

"My parents died. Roman and Ivan took me in."

"How did they die?"

Their eyes met in the mirror, and the girl replied, "Roman and Ivan."

19

The auditorium, which was part of Roman's castle, was entirely new to Torenia. She'd never been to a play or a ballet; none of the towns she'd traveled to had anything this stunning or grandiose. It had layers of seats in a bowl shape, cut off before the stage. The golden embellishments on the white walls were intricate swirls and patterns, each design made with care. The seats were a rich red, as were the carpets that lined the floors.

Centered directly at the back was the luxury seating, where only the richest could afford to sit. That was where Torenia found herself, far from the show, but able to view it without looking back and forth across the stage. There were binoculars for her viewing pleasure, and she could also see all the people below her, the human civilians with no idea there were vampires sitting behind them, fully aware of each pulse of the blood in their veins. The murmur of chatter filled the auditorium as they waited. Torenia wondered how many others were here.

In her black gown and gloves that extended beyond her elbow, she felt the chill of the air on her naked shoulders. There was no shawl to cover her; goosebumps dotted her exposed skin. On either side of her sat Roman and the empty spot reserved for Ivan; Roman insisted that she take the center seat, for this evening was entirely for her pleasure.

"Have you ever seen a ballet?" Roman asked.

"Where I am from, we hid behind walls and cast away the arts," she replied. "Nothing beautiful survived there."

"Is that why you left?"

A flush tinted her cheeks, flattery was something she did indulge in. "Perhaps."

"The red suits you," Roman said eyes briefly glancing to her lips. Then he averted his eyes to the empty stage, its massive black curtains still closed.

Behind them, Ivan wrenched open the red curtain that separated their private box from the hallway. Torenia turned to look, though Roman remained focused on the stage. Ivan had a smear of blood on his lip but, before she was able to comment on it, he licked his lips slowly, fully aware that she watched. A smile danced onto his moist lips, flashing his sharp teeth.

Torenia was thankful the blush had been on her cheeks prior to Ivan's flash of lust. Quickly, she turned her attention to the stage, wondering when the ballet would begin. She was eager to see such beauty, having heard what others had said about it. She'd never seen a dance in her life, and she felt utterly deprived after seeing the finery worn for such an event.

"Let the show begin," Ivan muttered under his breath, the tone of his voice suggesting he knew something the rest of them did not.

The curtains were drawn, and a dark stage was revealed. Slowly, out of the blackness, petite women emerged, dressed in tight white outfits with flared skirts. Their legs and arms were bare, and they moved in unison with flawless grace. The stage was their world, and they were in full control. Swirling around like an optical illusion, one girl became three; three became one. Then, from the back, men in form-fitting black outfits danced into the mix. The women were tossed and twirled; the trust between them was unbelievable to Torenia.

She sat on the edge of her seat as the orchestra played song after song, each one blending into the next. She could watch such beauty without break; the world could burn around her and she would not notice. Torenia had no concept of how much time had gone by when the performance concluded, but she watched in sadness as all the dancers disappeared from the stage, moving back into the darkness.

Turning to look at Roman, a glimmer of sadness in her eyes. She opened her mouth to speak when he raised his hand.

The dancers appeared in the crowd, plucking people from the inner seats down in the bottom of the bowl. They were brought to the stage, shaking with excitement—or was it fear? Torenia leaned over the edge of the balcony to get a better look with her opera glasses. With stilted movements, men and women went up onto the stage, complete opposites of the graceful ballerinas.

When a dozen people had gathered, a ballerina came to the front of the stage and said something too quietly for Torenia to hear.

Ivan leaned over and whispered in her ear. "She thanked the crowd for attending the *Blood Ballet* and for their sacrifice."

"Sacrifice?" Torenia turned to look at Ivan with a question, their eyes meeting for just a brief moment before he gestured to the stage.

She turned and watched as the dance and music began again; this time, the dancers were like predators. They lashed out at the victims on the stage, slashing at their throats as blood spurted from their victims' arteries. They moved too fast to keep up, their identical outfits making them look like one person moving too quickly for the naked eye to see. With each slash of flesh, blood spilled to the floor, staining their white skirts. The pale dancers were red with blood within minutes of this final dance. This was not about feeding; this was about power.

No one in the crowd screamed or rose from their seats to try and escape. But Torenia could see them shaking, sobbing, accepting. The violence was not a surprise to them, but it still terrified the people below.

"They offer sacrifice, and we offer them safety," Roman explained in a whisper. "There are Pure Blood armies out there who do not care about the survival of man. We understand, as Half Bloods, that our food source must continue and we can use them to help our armies flourish. The people in the city are under our protection, so long as they offer us a good show every now and then."

"A symbiotic relationship." Torenia nodded, impressed.

When she leaned back in her seat, she noticed Ivan was gone. The stage before them was being cleaned up, bodies dragged through the spilled blood off to the side. When it was empty, Ivan appeared center stage, his hands neatly tucked behind his back. The crowd went silent; no one even dared breathe. Torenia watched with fascination, impressed by the power that the brothers had over every person in the room.

"Thank you all for attending. Your sacrifice will be repaid by our fiercest protection." Ivan's grin was infectious. "Tonight, we have something special."

No one dared speak to their neighbor about what it might be. It was as though Ivan spoke to rows of statues.

"Tonight," he shouted, "I have brought you someone accused of the worst treacheries. Rape! Incest!" Ivan giggled slightly. "Our special guest is for our Sister, who will also be making her grand debut tonight."

Ivan spun on his heels, with his arm extended wide, as a man was brought onto the stage. He wore a black bag over his head, his hands tied together in front of him. Two bloodied ballerinas brought him in with ease, despite his frantic attempts to free himself. Forcing him to his knees, one of the ballerinas pulled the bag free. He had pale skin, reddened under his freckles. His hair was cut short, the color of it, a familiar crimson. Torenia's heart lurched.

"I present to you, Felix Răceanu." Ivan looked up through the rows of people directly at Torenia. "Will our Sister please come to the stage?"

Roman patted Torenia's thigh, a comforting gesture to follow Ivan's request. She stood and felt herself seething inside. This was the man who had raped Scarlett, his own sister, and gotten away with it. It was Scarlett who had paid the price, the cost weighing on her until the day she had been burned alive. Torenia disappeared from the luxury seats and was guided to the stage by a petite ballerina. Her hair was pulled back so tightly that her face was taut, masked with makeup and blood.

Torenia stood on the stage, looking at the quivering man before her, then looked at Ivan. He smiled at her, a grin that could scare anyone, but he did not frighten her. The Brothers had kept their promise to bring him to her. She faced the accused man, dressed in filthy rags while she wore the finest clothing she'd ever worn.

"Do with him what you will," Ivan told her, then stepped back, hands locked in front of his stomach.

Torenia wanted to rip his throat out, taste his tainted blood. She wanted to burn him alive, watch the skin peel from his face like his sister's. She wanted to make him suffer for the rest of his life. However, she suspected this was a test—but for what? How cruel she could be? Or was it a chance for them to see what she did when she was handed power?

She had the chance to take control, to give something back to the people who just lost loved ones, neighbors, friends.

She turned to the crowd. "You've all given so much tonight. My name is Torenia Luca, and I too have been given protection by Roman and Ivan Sokolov and the Brotherhood. The world is a cruel place, and they took me in. But not everyone is given such a promise of safety. This man," she gestured to him, "raped his own sister. When she became pregnant, she was blamed for seducing him. Cast out of her home, she had everything stripped from her. If she had protection as I do, as *we* do, she would still be here today.

"I ask you all to come up here—the face may be different, but the crime is the same. Every one of you has faced horrors, but we promise you protection. I will promise you vengeance upon those who harm you." People began to rise uneasily from their seats, coming to the stage, not even noticing Ivan standing there when they had shaken in fear of his presence only moments before. Torenia held their hands and brought them to the stage. "Come, come!"

"You have power too; now take it back," she said to those who braved the stage.

The first punch sent Felix back; he struggled to get upright without the use of his hands, begging for mercy. The second blow quickly followed and blood was spilled upon the stage again. The kicking and punching picked up, slurs and insults coming from the mouths of those who felt their autonomy had been taken from them by people like Felix. They all had their own monsters; Torenia simply gave them a face and body to destroy. While they fought demons in their head, taking it out on Felix, their attention was distracted from the real monsters—Roman and Ivan. It was the first command Torenia had proclaimed and, even from the stage, she could see that Roman was impressed.

Fascination consumed her as she watched the limbs being torn from Felix's body; she did not know if he was dead or not, but he would be soon. Satisfaction swept over her, and she was taken aback by her own enjoyment of this macabre event. Ivan's hand was on her shoulder to steady her. She glanced at the private box again and saw Roman staring coldly at him.

Ivan flashed a grin at his brother.

20

B ack within her room—which was larger than her family's house in Silvania—Torenia smiled at herself in the mirror. The image that she once saw in her mirror, which she used to scry with as a child, was now clear. Her bright red lips were perfectly shaped, and she knew it was her color. Dawn was fast approaching, and she longed to crawl into her soft bed and sleep until the moon rose. However, another part of her was wildly excited about what had occurred at the ballet. She had taken hold of a powerful leadership role, showing the people that the Brotherhood was in place to protect them all: the Pure Bloods, the Half Bloods, and the fodder.

They were blind to what was really going on. Though she hadn't yet seen the harvest, she had known of its existence before she arrived. Roman and Ivan had certainly set up something for themselves and for the food. The protection they offered was granted—to a degree. Nothing came free in this world; to offer up a few people, here and there, to keep them compliant was a brilliant scheme.

Torenia wished to see the harvest, for she doubted its quality. The blood had a strange taste since she'd arrived at the Brotherhood. Ivan had promised her he would show her the harvest and the library as well, which had made Torenia swoon. It was within the pages written by other witches that she would find a wealth of knowledge. She longed to learn, to become the strongest witch that there was.

A knock distracted her from her thoughts. "Enter!" she called without turning from her seat at the vanity.

Irina stepped in, bowing her head as she always did. "Would you like to disrobe, *Koroleva*?"

"Despite the beauty of the gown, I have been longing to get out of it since I put it on." Torenia smiled at the girl, then stood up so she could begin unlacing the corset. She couldn't help but think how much more satisfying it would be if someone, other than Irina, removed it. The girl was pretty, but much too young for Torenia.

The gown came off, and Torenia could breathe again, before putting on her robe; Irina pulled the pins from her hair, letting the black satin locks fall down. They reached the middle of her back, wavy from having been pinned up for so long. Irina grabbed the brush to begin smoothing out her hair. One hundred strokes, the golden number, whether or not the old adage was true. Torenia sat and faced the vanity again. It made the one hundred strokes easier to bear for her, though it made no difference to Irina. She still had to remain on her feet until Torenia decided she could rest.

"Roman instructed me to inform you that he was very pleased with the events that occurred at the bal-ballet." Irina's voice shook when she spoke of the Blood Ballet. "He expresses his pleasure to have someone with fine-tuned leadership skills at his side."

"Go on." Torenia knew that there was more. She looked into Irina's eyes through the mirror.

"He hopes you will join him, Ivan, and the other superiors at a tactics meeting so that you might further your leadership." She bowed her head, still stroking the brush through Torenia's hair.

"You are terrified of him. Ivan too. Are you scared of me?"

Irina stopped brushing. "*Koroleva*...I..."

"My dear, you are surrounded by people who would drink your blood like it was wine. You have the right to be scared."

Irina nodded.

"Why does he keep you human?"

"The inability to face the sun makes many tasks difficult for your ki—for vampires. To have human servants is very smart."

"Do you feel safe here?"

She nodded. "My parents gave their lives for mine."

"The ballet?"

Irina nodded again. "Roman promised them I would remain safe from all: man, vampire, bezou."

"You know of werewolves?" Torenia's interest was piqued.

"Oh, yes, the library here covers all sorts of species, sciences, and curious things." Irina had a bounce to her voice, a passion for learning. "I was in awe when I first saw it."

Nodding absentmindedly, Torenia grew silent for a moment, frowning. This child had seen the chasm of books and knowledge before she had. With a wave of her hand, she dismissed Irina. Alone again, she tightened the cinch on her robe and grabbed the candle holder. The flame sputtered from her quick movements but remained lit as she briskly traversed the crisscrossing hallways.

The giant double doors of the library were similar to those at the entrance of the castle, making a great noise as she pushed them open. The dark room smelled of dust and ancient secrets. Her tiny flame did nothing to alleviate the gloom, so she began to locate the lanterns, lighting them with her candle. Slowly, the shape of the room was revealed—giant towers of books, shelves on two floors, each more than ten feet tall. A stairwell curled around the center of the room, breaching the second floor. She stared in awe, realizing she had no idea where to start.

With one hand clutching the candlestick, she ran her finger over the spines of the books. Many of them were in pristine condition, others were ancient and crumbling. She didn't touch those for fear they would fall apart. Many of the titles were in languages she was unfamiliar with; some did not have titles at all.

Let it guide you, a voice echoed through Torenia's head. She jerked back in fright, expecting to see someone appear from behind a shelf. But, as she peered around and her heart rate slowed, she realized no one was there with her. She concluded that she had simply scared herself before moving on to search for a book. Something tugged her along the shelves.

A large brown book with some sort of skin for the binding caught her attention. Like a ghost was in the room, pointing her in the direction of that specific book, she felt drawn to it. Placing the candle on the shelf, she carefully began to pull the book from the shelf. Dust fell from its cover, no title on the spine or its cover. Opening it, she supported the heavy tome with her left forearm and thumbed through its pages.

"*Potio mortem,*" Torenia muttered. "The Death Potion"

She flipped to another section, jumping past large chunks of pages.

"*Laliges duplicia: animalia et homines,*" she read. "Binding: animals and humans."

This was the book she needed; it called to her for a reason. A compendium of witchcraft over the years. Pieces of magic, learned by hundreds of different witches, all recorded in a single tome. She peered at the shelf she had grabbed it from, wondering if there were others like it. It reminded her of the one Aster had years ago, but far more important. That had been stories and a handful of potions, nothing like the book in her hands. Witches from all over the world would have books like this, where their descendants could carry on penning their learnings. Torenia looked further, just one more page. What she saw there stunned her.

"*Maladictum Luca...*The Luca curse."

"Torenia, Torenia," Ivan's voice rang out, but it was muffled by the insulation of the masses of books. "You could not wait one more day?"

"Where did you get this book?" She turned to face him.

"I am a collector of many things. The more you know, the less can harm you."

"Yes, knowledge is power," she agreed. "But this book has a direct connection to me."

"How do you think we discovered you, Torenia?"

"I already told Roman I have no control over the Wolf. I have no daughters to sacrifice."

"It was never the Wolf we were interested in. Too many...caveats." He spoke for himself and Roman. "The curse led to the name Azalea Luca. The name led us to you."

Ivan stepped close to her, the orange glow of the lanterns making the shadows dance across his face; it was as though he had changed right before her eyes. He took the book from her hands and placed it on the shelf behind her, open to the page she had left it on. Facing her dead on, one hand still touching the book, the other hovering by her waist, a bubble of lust burst between them, not unlike the feeling she'd had with Adam all those years ago.

"There are other things that have power," he said, his voice swaying like a song. His well-manicured hand touched her thigh through her silk robe, sending jolts of electricity through her. It had been a long time since she had felt the touch of a man. His lips moved to her neck, kissing the supple skin there.

"If Roman found out..."

"He won't," Ivan promised.

"How long..." She moaned as his hands moved underneath her robe. "How long have you known about me?"

"Long enough to be fascinated by you." He nibbled her earlobe, then began to kiss down her collarbone, lower and lower.

Torenia untied the string that held her robe shut as Ivan knelt before her. His hand caressed her bare calf, guiding her leg over his shoulder. She leaned her head back against the shelves, a book tumbling off the other side as she allowed him to ravish her. Ivan's strong hand slid between her thighs. He clutched her flesh and brought his mouth to her skin. The sharpness of his teeth grazed her. Then, with a perfect jerk of his jaw, he broke the skin on her inner thigh. Blood beaded, slipping down her leg.

She moaned when he dragged his tongue over the blood, lapping at it. With gentle fierceness, he sucked at her skin, drinking a small amount of her blood. Her body shook with euphoria, yet he'd scarcely touched her. The feeling of Ivan sensually drinking her blood was starkly different from Roman turning her, and it filled her core with an ache for more.

She had Ivan right where she wanted him. With her hand, she

gripped his hair, pulling his head back so she could look into his brilliant blue eyes. There would have been a time when she thought he was absolute perfection, but she knew she now held that title. Her tongue darted out over her lips, and she narrowed her eyes. He grinned, moving from the small flesh wound he had caused to where she truly wanted him. As she moaned with bliss, she arched her back and leaned her head against the bookcase again, her hand still gripping his hair to keep him exactly where she wanted him.

As her pleasure built, she grabbed Ivan's hand and brought it to her mouth. Biting down onto his wrist, she punctured his flesh and began to drink his blood, rich with her own. The taste of her own kind, the taste of herself, pushed her over the edge as she gasped. She sucked the blood from his wrist again, a few more drops as she felt the waves of pleasure begin to slow.

Ivan untucked himself from under her leg, running his hands up along her ample hips and slender waist. His lips were crimson with the blood from her thigh. While his eyes were hungry before, they were starving now after tasting her.

She smiled wickedly, tying her robe closed with slightly trembling hands.

A look of betrayal crossed Ivan's eyes, then he grinned with a wickedness that almost matched Torenia's.

"You truly are meant to be a queen," he said, watching her as she left him desperate and hanging without another word.

Her brisk footsteps were silent along the halls of the castle, but her heart raced in her chest. The spying, the constant awareness that if she got caught, she would be killed in an instant. Regardless of the wrath, Roman would bring upon anyone who laid a finger on her, it broke her down into nothing more than a quivering husk of the girl she used to be. She'd chewed her nails down to the quick since she went from basic maid to Torenia's personal attendee. Despite not being two decades old, she saw gray hair sprouting in her thick locks.

This place was killing her.

Images of what she just witnessed flashed through her mind, confusing her. Part of her envied Torenia and the way she did not fear Ivan and Roman. The graceful way she disrobed without a flush reaching her cheeks, the way she took control of the situation. The way she made Ivan do what she wanted. Irina had never been touched that way.

She knocked on the door to Roman's study.

"Come in, Irina." His playful voice bounced off of the walls.

Irina entered the room, its walls painted a burnt red color. Black curtains covered the large windows, making the room dark except for the glow of the lanterns and the fire dancing in the hearth. Roman sat behind a table in a massive leather chair, its mate a few feet away. She stood shakily just inside the room, waiting for him to ask what he wanted to know. Her hands were clutched together behind her back, slick with sweat.

"Sit down, sit down." He gestured to a leather chair opposite the one he was in. When she was settled, he leaned forward, his ungloved hands a rare but terrifying sight. His long nails were a constant reminder of the damage he could do.

"Tell me," Roman commanded. His voice rose and fell, with playful emphasis on different words.

"She—"

Roman cleared his throat. "Who?"

"*Koroleva*. Apologies, *Korol*."

"Much better, do go on." Something danced in his blue eyes.

"*Koroleva* has discovered the book, just as you said she would," she told him, still uncomfortable in his presence. "But, *Korol*, she may have discovered something else."

Roman smiled wryly. "And what might that be?"

She glanced up and met his piercing blue stare, wondering if he truly wanted her to speak it. She blushed horribly, breaking away from his gaze in embarrassment and fear. "She and Ivan..."

Roman leaned back in his seat, hands now upon the arms of the chair. His gruesome nails tapped on the ends of the chair, scraping the leather. His eyes bore into the wall behind Irina's head, his expression completely unreadable.

To her relief, he would not kill the messenger. He waved her off like she was a fly bothering him. "You may go."

21

The massive arched windows in the meeting room allowed Torenia a view of the black night sky. Before her sat a giant oak table, the knotted wood perfectly sanded, but still visible beneath the varnish. The rough edges of the bark were glazed over, torn from nature but kept intact in the purest form possible. Torenia thumbed the rough bark, dark compared to the smooth top of the table, showing the decades the tree had lived. She sat to the left of Roman's seat—he had not yet arrived—with Ivan across from her.

There were seven other vampires in the room. Despite being called the Brotherhood, Torenia was pleasantly surprised to see three women amongst the leaders. Seeing this, she relaxed slightly. She reminded herself, as she sat almost at the head of the table, that she was new to all of this and had not yet earned the spot where she sat. Her thoughts trailed to Nikolai, the youngest brother, and wondered if he would ever return. If he did, would she lose her place here? She hoped her contribution to the Blood Ballet had solidified her role, but she was not naïve enough to believe it was secure yet.

"You must feel like a rabbit in the wolf's den," one of the women said, startling her. She was striking, with light blonde hair and gentle gray eyes. She stood beside Torenia's chair, bent over slightly so they could speak quietly beneath the chatter of the others in the room.

Torenia quickly composed herself. "I do not fear wolves."

The woman smiled, flashing her fangs in a hearty smile. "I respect that. You may not fear them but don't ever trust them. Not entirely."

Torenia raised an eyebrow.

"I'm Natasia. I've heard much about you already, Torenia. You are as beautiful as they say."

"They already speak of my beauty, but nothing else?" Torenia was both delighted and frustrated. "I apologize to say I've not heard of you, Natasia."

"Let your beauty misdirect them," Natasia said, flicking her hand casually. "I hope that, just as I have taught my daughter, Tasia, I can leave you with one lesson."

"And what might that be?"

"Use every weapon in your arsenal."

Torenia couldn't help but smile. "And this daughter of yours, will she grace us with her presence?"

"We alternate; our duties are shared equally."

"I envy that," Torenia admitted, immediately wishing she could take it back. She didn't know Natasia, so didn't know what might be reported back to Roman. "I never got on with my mother."

"You seem to be doing fine without her."

"Yes..." Torenia tapered off.

Natasia patted her shoulder, then sauntered to her seat with a sway to her hips.

A few standing members spoke in hushed tones until Roman entered the room. Within seconds of his eyes landing on them, the stragglers still standing took their seats, chastened by his icy blue stare. Torenia wanted that.

"So." Roman clapped his hands together, eyes scanning the table, pausing on Torenia. "First and foremost, I would like to introduce to you our Sister, Torenia."

Mumbled welcomes and heads being nodded politely took a few seconds, then there was silence again. Natasia broke it. "We heard very good things about you, and your spectacle at the ballet was very well received; we commend you for your leadership."

"Thank you, Natasia." Torenia nodded.

"Torenia could very well have saved us from an uprising by the people," Roman pointed out, directing the conversation back to the intended purpose. "If they were aware—and collected enough—they could easily overpower us. Already, Torenia has shown us a different kind of power. I would hereby wish to appoint her to all human resource-based issues and tasks. Does anyone oppose this?"

No one raised a hand.

"Very well."

"Congratulations, Torenia." Natasia's cold gray stare warmed.

"Now, we must address the attacks. Dmitry, I understand you have been *foul* since our youngest brother left—temporarily, might I add—and you wish to see a Pure Blood upon the throne," Roman said.

Dmitry rose from his seat, his black hair slicked back from his pale face. Roman's eyes narrowed at his challenger as Dmitry cleared his throat. "We will not kneel before Half Bloods, witches, and whores."

Natasia laughed, a shrill laugh that sliced through the murmurs. "Terrified of a woman on the throne, Dmitry, you old stiff? You do not see me crying about a bunch of Half Bloods on the throne. They keep us fed, they keep the people scared enough not to revolt, and quite frankly, not one of them is hard on the eyes. I would not be so opposed to," she cackled, "kneeling before them."

Roman looked like he was on the verge of ripping out every single vampire's throat in the room. Ivan leaned against the right side of his chair, grinding his thumbnail between his teeth, a smile permanently on his lips. He was enjoying every second of the chaos.

Torenia rose, managing to hide the fact that she was shaking. All of these people were more experienced and exposed to this world than her; she knew nothing of their politics. All of these people could kill her without difficulty, or they could vote her out and render her powerless. She was filling an important role and if she did not deliver, she knew they would cast her aside. However, she also knew she had Roman and Ivan to support her; no one would dare turn their back on them. Although, from the looks of it, some of them were close. Perhaps the Brotherhood was falling apart. Torenia kept this piece of information close; she would use it when the time was right.

"We will bring him home, the youngest brother," Torenia told them.

"Nikolai?" Natasia spoke up. "The boy does not have the stomach for what happens here. I say good riddance! He was not built for the world of vampires, even if he is a Pure Blood."

Torenia blanched, wondering if what Natasia was suggesting was that she was better suited. She turned to look at Roman to gauge his reaction, but what she saw there was only murderous intent. His blue eyes were narrowed into slits, jaw clenched.

Natasia's words were careless, a jest. But to Roman, they were treasonous. He stood silently, only his chair making a noise when he pushed it from beneath him. Swiftly and slowly all at once, as though Torenia was seeing it as a memory instead of in real time, he walked over to where Natasia was seated. Her eyes widened when she sensed his intent, his name bubbled out from her lips as she began to beg, but he did not waste any time. Standing behind her chair, before she could escape, he grabbed either side of her head and twisted, snapping her neck. The sickening crunch of bone echoed across the room.

It also echoed inside of Torenia's head, and she realized, moments later, that she was covering her mouth with her hands. Her first potential ally was gone; her trust in Roman wavered.

Ivan giggled when Roman let go, letting Natasia slump forward. Her head hit the table with a *thunk.*

Everyone else remained silent.

Once Roman returned to his place at the head of the table, he stood behind his seat with his hands gripping the backrest.

"Clean up your mess, Dmitry, or I will. The Pure Blood attacks will stop. You would much prefer handling it than having me deal with it, yes?" Roman demanded.

"Yes, *Korol.*" Dmitry sneered when he bowed his head.

Torenia shook. It had not gone unnoticed that Roman had done nothing when Dmitry had called her a whore, yet when Natasia insulted Nikolai, he went berserk. She was not on the same level as the brother who had abandoned them, and it made her blood boil.

"Ivan, bring Tasia her mother's body. Do not defile it." Ivan slouched. "Tell Tasia she is now in command of her sector."

Roman pointed at another man, one Torenia recognized. He was the one who had been watching her the night she met Roman. "Vlad, the harvest is running lower than I would prefer. Round up another culling."

"Yes, *Korol*." Vlad nodded and ducked out of the room, unfazed by the dead body.

"When Ivan returns from his task, he, Torenia, and I *will* retrieve Nikolai," Roman announced, eyes scanning the room again. No one dared move nor dared look at the corpse; Roman's word was final.

Torenia saw how far being feared got Roman, and she envied him for it. Having tried to take the honorable route to ensure all parties would be content, she had only succeeded in getting Natasia killed. She had been one of Roman's supporters, but he had not hesitated to kill her when she spoke ill of Nikolai. Torenia would not have batted an eye if anyone said cruel things about Aster, and she began to envy the relationship that the brothers had.

Despite him leaving them, Ivan and Roman still loved their brother.

22

I t was the sunset she missed, but the night had always been her protector. Sunrise always reminded Torenia of her hometown, of rising early enough to see the sun stretch over the horizon. It meant work, chores, and abuse. Cruel words from her mother and sister, and neglect from her father. Sunset, however, meant the day was done and night was coming to wrap her in its embrace, protecting her. Hidden in the darkness, she could creep into the wardrobe to hide away and pretend she was the most beautiful woman in the world.

With her gaze upon the stars and the moon, she reminisced about the sunset she would never see again. A cold chill nipped her bare shoulders as she surveyed the garden, but she did not reach for her shawl. Entranced by the beauty of the night—something she never truly embraced like this until she had been turned into a vampire— she dared not move, as though she might disturb its peace.

In the castle behind her came gentle sounds—chattering maids and the odd clatter of something falling to the ground. But it was otherwise silent. Even though the castle was massive, only Roman, Ivan, Torenia, and the maids called it home. Though it was not full of people, it was full of secrets, hidden within the books, hidden in the very walls.

Rahella quorked in the distance, appearing out of the darkness moments later. She was nearly impossible to see until the lantern light cast an orange shade across her slick wings. Landing on Torenia's outstretched arm, the bird shut her eyes in satisfaction. Her witch was safe, she had completed another task for the day. No longer needing to guide Torenia, the old familiar was simply a dear friend. Rahella still had her uses, but Torenia allowed her to be as free as she could be.

"My sweetest friend," she said in a sing-song voice. "I think it is time for some light reading, yes?"

Rahella made a soft noise in agreement.

Torenia looked at the giant book, bound in flesh, and wondered how many witches had written in it, how many had it been handed down to, generation by generation. Or how many, like her, had found the book and learned the Craft from it? Would she eventually pen her own concoctions of death in its pages? She ran her hand along the smooth cover, almost flawless if not for the age that cracked its binding. She had already read a few sections, though some of it was in a language she did not understand, and some were so faded that the spells had been erased by time.

Every book she had found said the same thing: earth magic was the core of all magic. Every witch, whether deep in the art or dabbling on the surface, relied on what the earth gave them. Blood magic was more potent; it added immeasurable strength to all curses, hexes, and bonds. Moon magic was another, though difficult to work with because the moon was always changing. Everything had to be perfect when it came to moon magic, so few witches worked with it. Not everyone could wait for the right cycle of the moon to cast a curse; sometimes, there was no time.

"How to stop time." Torenia posed the idea, pondering it, tasting it. In her mirror dreams as a youth, she saw herself as she was now. But no older.

"Torenia, Torenia, Torenia." Ivan appeared from behind a perfectly cut hedge, a wicked grin on his face that warmed his stunning blue eyes.

"Good evening, Ivan." She glanced up at him. It had been a few weeks since the tactics meeting, longer since their encounter in the library. His task to return Natasia's body to her daughter completed, he was back at the castle.

"I would like to show you the harvest." He reached for her hand.

Torenia looked longingly at the book in her lap; she had been waiting some time to really pore over its contents. She needed to become not only the witch that Roman wanted but the one she needed to be as well. All that knowledge in one book; it reeked of power, and she longed for a taste. With that knowledge, she would one day take over what Roman currently held.

"The book will still be there when we are done," he reminded her.

She sighed. Rahella propped herself atop the book as though promising Torenia she would guard it with her life. She relaxed slightly and accompanied Ivan. They walked through the gardens, covered in the bright white snow of winter. It fell endlessly from the gray clouds carpeting the world.

Inside the castle was warm, but there was a different kind of heat as they took the stairs down to the basement. Torenia never wandered this far, for she had no desire to visit this part of the castle. She could smell sweat and something rank from the top of the steps but continued to follow Ivan down the twisting, narrow stairwell. Shouts and pained moans reached Torenia's ears, a veil of dirty air consuming her.

At the bottom of the stairs was a wrought iron door. Ivan withdrew a key from his pocket and opened the lock; shouts and whimpers followed the loud clang of the door. Rows upon rows of tiny cages, with one person per cage, filled the room. There was not enough room for an average-sized person to sit down. Their bare flesh was filthy, pock-marked, and hacked at. Torenia could smell the blood; it aroused her hunger. Her tongue darted out instinctively, even if the sight disgusted her. She'd lived on a farm long enough to know that even the best-treated animals sensed that they would be slaughtered eventually. Studying all these terrified people, she realized they had not lost hope. They reached their thin arms between the bars of their cages and grabbed for her, but they were unable to reach her.

It was disgusting, but she was eager to see more. After all, this was where her food came from.

Ivan walked ahead, a bit of a hop to his step, beckoning for her to follow without looking back. She walked behind him and through another locked door after passing four dozen cages on either side. The cages must have run the entire length of the castle, she thought, but something far more disturbing waited beyond the second locked door.

Five devices held naked men and women upside down, leather clamps attached to their feet. Their arms dangled, tubes connecting at the radial and carotid arteries; the blood from their near-lifeless bodies drained into buckets. Two of the three women looked at Torenia, their mouths opening and closing like a fish, but they could not speak. Torenia knew they were asking for help.

The man at the end was dead, his body fully drained. Ivan pulled the three tubes from his body and lifted the furthest bucket, bringing the rusted metal lip to his mouth and guzzling down its contents.

He set the bucket back down and groaned with satisfaction.

Torenia knew the feeling, for she craved it too. Reaching for the bucket, she grabbed it and drank deeply. The fresh blood was delicious but not as good as taking it directly from the body. Unlike a fine wine, it did not need to sit or be aerated; it was best from the throat. She had been given endless cups of blood since her arrival here; any time she became hungry, Irina would arrive with more blood to satisfy her. The harvest was a necessity, she understood that. Vampires could not go out hunting every night; suspicions would grow too quickly. Man would eventually riot.

"If the people find out about this, they will revolt."

"Who would dare come close enough to find it?" he replied, gesturing to the cages. "These are the worst of the worst: rapists, killers. It was Nikolai's suggestion that we harvest them. Although my dear baby brother killed only the wretched, he also considered himself one of them."

"And what do you consider our kind?" Torenia asked, the blood settling in her stomach and easing her hunger.

"You and I see the world differently, Torenia. When others see carnage, we see beauty. When others see a massacre, we see elegance. What others consider horrible, we consider exquisite. We are exquisite."

Torenia felt an odd sense of understanding when he spoke those words.

"You see, it used to be all criminals...but we ran out of those and had to improvise," he explained with a nod to explain some of the younger people hanging upside down.

"I hardly doubt there is a shortage of criminals," Torenia replied. Her tone dripped with venom.

He flashed her a brief smile, brushing off her words, before continuing. "I got you a gift, *Koroleva*." He dug into his jacket's inner pocket, withdrawing a small box.

Taking it from his hands, Torenia held the small, jet-black box. It was practically weightless. As she opened it, she was surprised to find a necklace on a silver chain. Dangling from the chain was a pendant, perfectly tear drop shaped, a dark red that glimmered like a ruby.

"This is beautiful." She pulled the necklace out of the box and held it up to the light.

"It is made from the blood of Felix Răceanu, what little I was able to scrounge from the stage after the Blood Ballet."

Her eyes met Ivan's, and both of them were filled with wickedness and desire for all things *exquisite*. She knew then what it would take to best everyone who had taken from or tried to use her, including Roman.

23

A piano stood in the throne room; Ivan sat, playing a beautiful melody, much to Torenia's surprise. It echoed through the entire room, filling her with unbound elation. He moved with a grace she did not realize he possessed, as if the music controlled him and he was its puppet on a string.

Roman sat beside Torenia, though his throne was the tallest. Rahella perched on the back of Torenia's seat as the music connected all of them; it felt as though they were a normal family listening to their loved ones entertain them. The only disturbance came when the great hall doors opened, and Vlad entered the room. He was thinner, his cheekbones jutting out either side of his dull eyes. His gait was confident but tired, suggesting that he had found what he was looking for. Or whom.

Removing his hat, Vlad bowed his head to Roman and Torenia while Ivan continued to play the piano in the background, listening but appearing aloof.

"*Korol, Koroleva*—"

"We are your equals," Roman corrected him, inviting him to join them.

Vlad nodded, eyeing Torenia with suspicion. "I have found Nikolai."

"Go on," Roman said.

"As you suspected, he is still with your mother. He spends the evenings in bars, drunk almost every night. He does not stray far from her side. You will need to strike soon."

"I think it is time we paid our mother a visit. What do you think, Ivan?" Roman asked.

Ivan did not stop playing but changed the tune as he sang, "Mother Dearest, to my heart you are nearest."

Roman clapped his hands together. "That settles it."

With bags packed for the journey south, they set out to find Nikolai and bring him home. Torenia sat in the back of the carriage, which was spacious and well-kept, alongside Roman and Ivan. The curtains were drawn back to allow the faint light from the moon that barely peaked through the clouds. The snow was ebbing at last as winter neared its end and spring approached. The nights were getting longer, making for shorter travel time, but Roman had appointed two men to guide the horses throughout the day and night. Rarely did the men have time to rest; it was to their benefit to push the horses for a quicker arrival time.

"Tell me about your brother," Torenia said.

Roman and Ivan looked up and met her gaze, unsure how to proceed.

Roman addressed her curiosity. "Nikolai was born a vampire. After our father was turned, he turned the rest of us: Mother, myself at seven, Ivan at five. Nikolai was born a vampire; Mother kept him to herself, for he was pure. Ivan and I obliged her but believed this inequality and cruelty were unfair. We sought a way to create balance and equality among all vampires."

"How righteous," Torenia replied, meaning every word.

Ivan chuckled. "Nikolai is righteous to the core. But a hypocrite. He slaughtered thousands of Half Bloods and Pure Bloods, even more men. Then, when we had achieved greatness and formed the Brotherhood, he ran."

"Watch your tongue, brother," Roman warned. "Nikolai has always been the *sensitive* one. He gets that from our mother, from the love she gave him, instead of us. He does not agree with the Blood Ballet, the executions, capital punishment of those who dare defy us, the harvest—even if he implemented some of our methods. What he does not understand is that equality cannot be achieved without blood."

"He believes violence begets violence?" Torenia asked.

"Precisely."

"Let me try to convince him," she suggested. Though this was partially for her own benefit, Nikolai might be able to give her a new insight, a new angle on how to break Roman when the time was right. "A fresh face, a friendly one. I may be able to convince him to return with the promise of a slight change. If he sees that you have allowed someone like me to take his place, perhaps he will believe you have changed or that you are open to change."

"Someone like you, dear?" Roman raised his eyebrow ever so slightly.

"In all my time traveling, it was you who looked beyond the fact I am a woman. You saw me for my ability, not for anything else. You made me a queen, but not *your* queen."

"If anyone can convince our baby brother, it is her," Ivan pointed out, flashing his teeth in a grin, eyes locked on Torenia. "Although he has a thing for blondes."

Roman stiffened slightly. "Torenia is our equal and will not be used as bait, nor as a whore. I hope I do not need to remind you of that again, Ivan."

"No," Ivan held Roman's stare, "you do not."

The cramped carriage air was stale. It drove all three of them to the brink of madness, forcing them to take a break. Torenia was the first to step outside. A fire was lit, revealing little of the scenery around them. Trees and earth—simple, and yet she could feel the earthen power beneath her feet. Touching the ground always brought her back to her senses.

Roman sat at the edge of the carriage, flask in hand, staring into the small flame. Ivan slipped around his older brother and hopped down, the carriage groaning from the loss of his weight, as though it breathed in, so it seemed to rise. Roman's face remained blank.

Ivan stretched his arms over his head, then rolled his shoulders and cracked his neck. "Fancy a walk, *Koroleva*?"

"I do," Torenia replied, her gaze flickering towards Roman.

"Don't go far," Roman told them, reaching behind and grabbing the lantern before handing it to Ivan. "If I can't see the lantern—"

"Don't act like you're my father, Roman," Torenia snapped before Ivan could get a word in. "I'm perfectly capable of handling Ivan."

"I'm well aware."

Ivan's grin looked ghastly in the lantern light. Torenia ignored him, staring down Roman. She wondered what he knew of her incident with Ivan in the library and if he was jealous. He didn't seem like the type of man who became jealous.

"I'll play by your rules, but only because I choose to." Before Roman could respond, Torenia turned her back on him. Distancing herself from their camp, she walked with her head held high. She could hear the brothers speaking, their voices heated, but could not make out their words. Moments later, she heard Ivan's hurried footsteps behind her, like a dog at her heels.

When he was at her side, she glanced at him. "Why *does* he care?"

Ivan shrugged. "Roman thinks I'll defile you."

"You'll do nothing to me without my command."

Ivan licked his lips. "I'd grovel at your feet if you commanded it."

"He does not know, does he?"

"Know what?" Ivan asked.

Torenia rolled her eyes. "About the library."

"I did not divulge our debauchery to him if that is what you're asking."

Torenia's shoulders dropped, releasing the tension. Ivan was easy to manage and manipulate. As Natasia had recommended, she was using every weapon in her arsenal. She could lord her beauty over him, command him with a crook of her finger. However, she had to do so with utmost caution—she did not want Roman to think she and Ivan might unseat him. Knowing his certainty to switch at a moment's notice, she didn't trust that Roman wouldn't do to her what he had done to Natasia.

"I hope you didn't ask me to walk with you for anything other than walking," Torenia said, feeling lighter now that she was out of Roman's sight. She could still see the small fire, keeping it in her sight so she wouldn't get lost. "Tell me how to convince Nikolai to return."

"I do not believe you will succeed," Ivan replied and, when he saw Torenia's disdain, carried on. "Natasia was right, Nikki was never built for our way of life."

"Then why does Roman wish him back?"

"The same reason any of us would—many have told him he won't succeed."

Torenia understood that, at least. "And if we can't convince him?"

"We have...contingencies in place."

Torenia didn't know what that could mean for Nikolai, but she didn't press further, hoping she could convince him to return. From what she'd heard about him, he was soft. Perhaps having him around would benefit her, giving Roman another focus so that she could solidify her role in the Brotherhood. Thoughts of the changes she would make followed her on the walk back, burrowing underneath her skin as they continued the last leg of their journey.

The tension lingered in the carriage and followed them for the remaining days and nights it took to reach their destination. Weeks had passed since they had left the Brotherhood. Now there was a warm wind coming from the south, bringing with it the feeling of spring. However, a chill remained between the brothers as they arrived. Taking shelter at an inn, no different from any of the ones Torenia had hopped between for many years, they each had their own room.

"The tavern is below," Roman told Torenia as they left her at her door. "Ivan and I will be going to our mother's home; a family reunion is in order."

"What will you be doing there?" Torenia asked.

"This matters not, my dear," Roman chided her. "What matters is that you keep Nikolai here for some time, until midnight at the earliest. I will not ask you to remain here when he returns home; if you wish to join us for the spectacle, you are more than welcome."

Ivan craned his neck backward, a sharp crack followed by a groan of satisfaction filling the empty space of the room. A carnal and hungry look lingered in his eyes, but it was not bloodlust—not the kind that kept him full and energized. No, he felt a different kind of lust, and Torenia found herself aching for him. She would not speak of it, especially not in front of Roman; she would never let a man have that power over her again.

"If I convince him to return, do you still wish for him to return to your mother's?" she asked cautiously, not wanting to make any mistakes here.

Roman had a look in his eye that told her he knew something she did not, but he did not reveal what it was. Closing the space between them, he lifted his gloved hand and cupped her cheek. Warmth radiated from him, but a chill ran the length of Torenia's spine when his icy glare lanced right through her. He leaned over and kissed each of her cheeks, then stood upright again.

"Yes, my dear. And I would love it if you came as well."

Ivan's eyes narrowed, jealousy radiating from him.

24

B ack in the familiar surroundings she had long forgotten, Torenia sat at the bar with a goblet of smooth wine in her grasp. She had been pleased to discover that she could still drink, even after the change. Slightly nervous, her hands were slick on the stem of the glass. Dipping her finger into the wine, she ran her finger along the rim of the glass to take off the edge. It played a soft lull, just loud enough for her to hear over the noise of the tavern. Part of her expected to wake up from this dream, the adventure she had undertaken since Roman had first approached her. It would not surprise her if some young woman approached to ask for her assistance for some ailment or another, or for help with an abusive husband.

But she was not approached by another woman; something about her aura turned people away from her, as though they could sense she was a predator. No one looked at her aside from sidelong glances. She did feel one pair of eyes on her back and, for the entire time she sipped her wine, they did not stray. Very few people had the ability to make her feel uneasy for no good reason. But she refused to be prey.

Finishing her wine, she held off buying another and left the counter to sit down at one of the tables where she could survey the room; she would recognize Nikolai if he looked anything like his brothers. The moment she turned around to find a table, she saw his brilliant blue eyes. He looked so much like his brothers, though slightly softer around the edges. His messy blonde hair was shaved along the sides, revealing his Brotherhood tattoos; a pint of ale sat before him, barely touched. Finding him was so easy it made her pause. Was this another test? She lingered for a moment too long; they made eye contact.

She studied him with a smile on her face, and his expression turned to confusion and interest.

Tentatively, she maneuvered the tables and drunk patrons of the tavern to stand at the edge of his table. Her fingertips pressed against the smooth wood and she looked down at the youngest Sokolov brother. She wondered, for a moment, if she really wanted him to return; she had everything she ever wanted because of his cowardice.

"My apologies, have we met before?" Torenia asked, feigning intrigue when really she was figuring out exactly what she was planning to do. What steps was she going to take to ensure her spot on the throne, to be the Sister among the Brothers?

"I would recognize your face if I had laid eyes upon you before," Nikolai spoke softly, with an edge of confidence. He had no idea who she was, and he had no clue that his brothers were waiting for him. "I'm Nikolai."

"Flattery will only get you so far, Nikolai." She smirked. "But do go on."

"Please," Nikolai gestured to the vacant chair, "have a drink with me."

"It would be my pleasure." She took the seat facing him and, extending her hand, introduced herself. "I am Torenia."

"A fine flower," he replied.

"You know your flowers?"

"My mother loves to garden. I presume yours did, as well?"

She scoffed, a bitter taste on her tongue, "My mother couldn't nurture anyone or anything."

"Do you have a surname, Torenia?"

She hesitated for a moment. "Luca."

His face didn't betray his thoughts. "You're not from here, are you?" he inquired curiously. He hid it behind the pint, downing a fair amount of the alcohol.

"Silvania," she replied. "Although I've been traveling around Osleka for many years."

"What brought you so far North?"

"Necessity."

"And what necessity was that?"

"To escape my binds, to find more in this world, to become more."

"Did you ever find that?" Nikolai thumbed the cold condensation coming from his ale. Around them, the world moved on; the bustle of the busy bar paid no mind to the two vampires seated at the table. Music played, mugs thunked down on tables, and barmaids rushed through the flurry of people, gathering empty mugs and collecting crude remarks and unwanted caresses.

"I found so much more. Power, riches, eternal beauty—"

Nikolai stiffened, his blue eyes darting around the tavern. His hand tightened around the glass. There was blood on his knuckles, dried and cracked. Fresh blood oozed from the newly exposed cuts, sliding around the mountainous grooves of his hand. Taking a deep breath, he turned his attention back to Torenia. Curiosity had been sharply replaced with distrust.

"It's a lie, all of it," he growled.

"What is?" Torenia asked. She knew he was referring to Roman and what he had promised her, but she wanted to know what he meant by his accusations. He knew Roman better than she did; she had to accept that. What Roman offered her was grand; she trusted him to a degree and would stand beside him, but she knew every last drop of information was vital to how she would play the game.

Nikolai's lip raised menacingly. "They sent you, didn't they? A pretty face to convince me to come back? I'm not going back."

Torenia's cover was blown; her expression hardened like a marble statue. She decided to tell Nikolai what Roman wanted him to hear. "Nikolai, they need you."

He let out a defeated sigh. "Whatever he has promised you, he's lying. You cannot trust Roman, and you certainly cannot trust Ivan. Listen, Torenia. I see goodness in you, and I do not wish to see another person dead because of me. I cannot..." he inhaled sharply, "I cannot have any more blood on my hands. Please, please run far."

"Nikolai." She reached her hands out in a motherly gesture, protective. "I have lived my entire adult life on the run. My family cast out anyone who is different. My cousin Mihai was nearly killed because he was different. The last I heard, he had to move as far as Kæ'vale just to avoid his murder—at the hands of his family. My family. Your family...they strive for equality. I am accepted there, regardless of status. I understand the ruthlessness is frightening, but I intend to make changes."

"He didn't..." Nikolai leaned across the table and grabbed Torenia's cheek before she could recoil, his thumb lifting her lip. When he saw her fangs, he leaned back in defeat. "You're just another toy."

"Roman has not laid a hand on me." She scowled.

"Roman doesn't lay his hands on anyone, not like that," Nikolai retorted. "No, he takes on challenges; it is how he keeps himself entertained."

"I am not a challenge to be conquered. Quite honestly, Nikolai, I sit where you should be, and I quite like it," she hissed. "Your return may very well jeopardize *my* place among your brothers."

"There, that right there." He shook his head. "You're scared he will toss you aside the moment he grows bored of you. And he will, Torenia. So, either run or make yourself indispensable."

She mulled over his words. Nikolai knew Roman and Ivan better than she ever would, but he was also blinded by bias. She had not yet proven herself indispensable, but she knew exactly how she could achieve that. She was making her mark.

Fueled by anger, she hoped it was midnight as she spat out the words. "You better run home then, Nikolai. I fear Roman and Ivan have not yet grown bored of you and will pay whatever price to force your hand."

Fear struck him; he rose so quickly that his thighs bumped the underside of the table. The pint glass wobbled, golden ale spilling over the lip of the glass. As the puddles formed, Nikolai grabbed his coat from the back of the chair. With a forlorn look on his face, he spoke softly. "Run, Torenia, while their attention is on me."

He mumbled as he walked away. "It's your only chance."

25

Following Nikolai on foot, Torenia's boots sank into the slushy remains of the winter snow. The path was muddy, full of rocks and grime. Clumps below the slush were frozen solid from never having seen sunlight, and they formed warped pieces of ice that jutted out, making a brisk pace near impossible. Overhead, Rahella soared along without any difficulty; Torenia envied her at that moment. With the safety of the inn behind her and the town no longer in sight, she pursued Nikolai—at a safe distance—through the woods.

It was a shortcut, she presumed, and it made walking even harder. Her night vision was excellent since she became a vampire, but it still did not hold a candle to seeing in daylight. She heard a shout, a deep voice crying out as light gleamed from the ramshackle house just ahead. Quickening her pace, she reached the front lawn where garden beds waited to be planted when the frost finally went away.

Nikolai's frantic shouting could be heard from the back of the house, and she could see a giant lake in the distance. It stretched far beyond the horizon, placid in the darkness, blending with the starless sky. When she entered the house, she saw Roman and Ivan seated in the main room, looking too large for the modest chairs.

"Torenia, I am so glad you could make it," Roman was soaked

from his chest down; water pooled around him on the floor, covering the wood. His hair was a mess, which was very unlike him.

"I am sorry I could not convince him—"

Roman waved a hand casually. "He would never be convinced, though I admire your dedication. He needed to be broken."

Roman gestured for her to look through the doorway into the backyard. A small figure in the distance knelt down, hunched over—Nikolai. He faced the water, holding something—someone. Torenia squinted to see better, but in the dark, it was almost impossible. She could only make out a white dress and long blonde hair touching the ground.

"You killed your mother?" Shock ran through her, and she thought back to her own family, wondering if they had all succumbed to some horrible plague like they deserved.

"Nikki killed Father, Roman killed Mother." Ivan cackled. "I am feeling very left out."

"Perhaps you will have the chance to kill our brother." Roman began to remove his gloves. "At the very least, you can *subdue* him."

"Here he comes now." Ivan lolled his head back over his shoulder, gazing out the window.

Nikolai walked with rage-fueled force, but a broken look was etched onto his face. His blonde hair was askew, mouth agape in shock, and his hands clenched into tight fists as he neared the house, Torenia stepped aside so she would not be part of the physical altercation that might occur. Wildly yanking the door open, Nikolai stormed in. The tears he shed for his mother stained his cheeks.

Nikolai went straight for Roman. The older brother rose from his seat and swiftly brought his fist around, making contact with Nikolai's jaw and knocking him to the ground. Nikolai twisted his waist and landed with both hands planted on the ground. When he tried to rise, Roman stomped on his hand, ripping a scream from Nikolai's throat as the bones crunched. Standing over his little brother, Roman knelt down and grabbed his collar. Lifting him halfway off the ground, he pounded Nikolai's head, one strike after the next, without a single break between blows.

Blood splattered from Nikolai's mouth, a tooth clattering to the ground. Nikolai groaned in pitiful defeat. Standing over him, Roman released his hold, dropping him back onto the bloody ground. He wasn't done, though, and grabbed Nikolai's broken jaw, causing him to cry out as blood pooled in his mouth. Roman's hands were covered in red as he leaned down to kiss his brother's cheeks before smearing them with his blood.

"You have been replaced, brother. I fought for you, defended you when others called you weak. But you *are* weak. You are a coward. Cowards do not deserve to live in this world. Just like the winter kills the weak, so will I."

Torenia had thought from the beginning that this had been about bringing Nikolai back. Now, she realized it was all to break him. Suddenly, his warning flashed in her head. Perhaps he was right—perhaps she was just a challenge for Roman, something to keep him from getting bored. No matter what, she had to stay on her toes and calculate every move she made to stay ahead of Roman.

He is key to the balance," a ghost of a woman's voice whispered in her head, the voice Torenia had heard in the library so long ago. She flinched slightly but understood the words. Despite not knowing who the voice belonged to, Torenia suspected that listening to it would help her achieve what she wanted.

"Wait," Torenia commanded. Roman stopped and stared at her; Ivan had wide eyes and a brilliant grin.

Torenia knelt beside Nikolai and Roman, having no idea how she got there. She could not stand by and watch Roman beat the life out of Nikolai, not after he had shown genuine concern for her well-being. There was a goodness in Nikolai that neither Roman nor Ivan possessed. Though it was something Torenia did not envy, she did not want to see it disappear from the world. Nikolai had a greater purpose, even if she wasn't sure what it was yet. She felt she owed him a chance to survive. His warning had to be rewarded.

"Stay out of this, Torenia," Roman snapped suddenly.

"If I am his replacement, I will have a say," she sneered. "If I am truly an equal, I deserve this."

"And what do you suggest we do with him, *Sister?*" Roman's eyes were crazed, showing the unhinged side of him that she had only glimpsed in fragments.

"You have just killed his mother—"

"My mother, too." Ivan pouted, a cheeky look in his eyes.

"Shut up, Ivan," Roman commanded.

"Give him time to recover. He knows who is in power, he knows it is not him. Now that he has no family other than you and Ivan, he will come crawling back."

"You did not go crawling back to your family, did you?" Roman asked, but it was clear he was cracking; he did not truly wish to kill his brother. Not yet, at least.

"I ended up with you."

Roman let go of Nikolai, who was fading in and out of consciousness. Blood dribbled from his slack jaw and his eyes rolled back in his head. Roman scowled down at his brother. He backed away from him, ignoring the disappointed look Ivan gave him.

"Come back, Brother," Roman spat, stepping over the semi-conscious Nikolai. Ivan fell in line behind Roman as he walked towards the door, Torenia following behind them. Roman stopped at the door, looking past them to glare at Nikolai. "Or finish the job you started."

Ivan giggled when they were out of the house, leaving behind a broken Nikolai. "Oh Torenia, Roman was only doing him a favor."

"A favor? How?" she asked, Roman far ahead of them now.

"Sweet Nikki tried to kill himself not long ago, but he failed. Perhaps this time, he will succeed."

26

"He is gone, *Korol*." Vlad knelt before Roman, seated upon his throne.

"*This is good*," the voice said to Torenia. As it was becoming more frequent, especially since meeting Nikolai the month before, Torenia had learned to listen and no longer jumped when she heard it.

Roman's gloved hands draped over his thighs, index finger twitching just enough to distract her. He leaned forward, a scowl on his normally inexpressive facial features. Having been delivered the news that Nikolai had run away like a coward, Roman was unable to contain his disdain. She had given Nikolai the chance to escape, she had convinced him to leave Nikolai behind. Their trust was now crumbling to nothing but ash. Turning his head slowly, Roman glared at her, ensuring that she knew she had crossed a line.

A month had passed since they had returned from their mother's, and the brothers had been waiting for Nikolai to desperately come crawling back, in need of family. But he had surprised them all by running away like a coward.

"Where?" Roman demanded answers.

"I asked everyone in the city; one woman, under duress, said she and Nikolai had relations...you know—"

"Yes, *I know.*" Roman's seething hatred for Vlad, and likely Torenia, could be felt in the air, stifling her ability to breathe.

"Said he came to her, broken jaw, broken *spirit*. She helped him get on his feet, and then he was gone," Vlad said. "Your mother was buried in the backyard, but there was no sign of Nikolai."

"Did you check the house?"

"The woman's?"

"Yes," Roman snarled.

"Of course." Vlad smirked. "Stayed for dinner, too."

"You may go, Vlad." Roman's jaw was tight. "Ivan, leave us."

Ivan's face flashed with concern, the first time Torenia had noticed an emotion aside from carnality in his eyes. This terrified her, for she would now have to face Roman for her mistakes; she had seen what he was capable of doing for the most minute of wrongdoings, what he was willing to do to family, to blood. She watched with a pained expression as Ivan stood up and walked down the stairs to the main level, wrapping his arm around Vlad's shoulder in a friendly gesture.

Silence enveloped the throne room after the doors slammed closed behind them. Knowing that she was to address Roman, she turned to face him. He was already staring at her, leaning sideways in his seat. His head barely turned, but his eyes bored through her, anger radiating off of him.

"Look what you have done."

Torenia did not stand down. "I truly believed he would return. You must have, too."

"Do not speak for me," he spat. "Mercy, and the pitiful fallacy of emotions you harbor have cost me my brother."

"Consider my lesson learned, how can—"

Roman cut her off. "Perhaps we need another to replace you." His hands clenched into fists on his lap.

As if the words surprised him, he seemed to ponder them, rolling them over and over in his head, considering the feasibility of finding someone who could replace Torenia. She could see it in his eyes, his fingers fiddling in his lap.

A glazed look fell over his eyes like a thin veil as the answer hit him. From the glare that followed, she realized he was quickly concluding that she was replaceable. Nikolai's words rang in her head; she had to make herself indispensable.

She glared at him. "No."

"Then reach your potential, before I grow tired of housing you while you are nothing more than a leech."

Roman grew increasingly unstable by the moment and, alone in the throne room with him, Torenia no longer felt safe. He was more unhinged than she had initially realized; the stress of the Brother-hood threatening to crumble and the weight of Nikolai wriggling out of his grasp... It was wearing him thin. She could see it in the way he spoke, moved, the way he led. She only had two plausible options— to prove her worth, and that her power could not be matched, or to run.

She refused to run any longer.

"May I leave? There is work to be done," she asked, desperate to get far away from Roman. She would not run away like Nikolai had wanted her to, but she did wish to flee to the library and focus on achieving her potential.

She hated how much Roman reeked of intimidation.

She envied it too.

"One more request," Roman said, suddenly calm and collected.

In the blink of an eye, he went from unhinged to a leader once again. People would kneel and bow, call him King and Brother. Vampires around the country shook in fear at his name, and Torenia understood why. He was not someone to be double-crossed, lied to, or disobeyed. She wondered if he knew what her plan was all along, her desire to be the one on the highest throne, the one to whom people bowed. She thought of Azalea Luca, a woman willing to betray anyone to get to the top, even her own kin. But what good had it done her?

Torenia would not be tied to a pyre and burned. She had to be smarter than her ancestors. "Anything," she said at last.

"Stay away from Ivan." His knowing eyes dug under her skin, exposing her secrets.

She suppressed the shock from showing on her face. Though she suspected Roman knew, she wondered how he had learned this information. Her mind reeled, cogs and gears turning as she ran through the list of possibilities. It suddenly became quite clear to her, but she remained stoic, saying nothing in reply. There was no one who could know about what had happened between them in the library—aside from Ivan and herself. Above all else, for a reason she could not figure out, she had trusted Ivan would keep that secret between them.

"Who told you?" There was no sense in lying about what Ivan and she had done.

"That does not matter," he said.

Torenia narrowed her eyes, piecing together who might have stumbled upon them that night in the library. Who wandered quietly and came to Torenia's beck and call? Who was never far away, ready to come at the ring of a bell? Who was under Roman's employ and would do as he asked, putting his demands above what Torenia requested?

"He was told not to lay a hand on you," Roman continued when Torenia didn't reply. "He disobeyed."

"Why does it matter who I am involved with? Unless you are interested?" she replied, truly curious why he was so opposed to her sexual endeavors with Ivan.

"My dear, I am not interested in anyone," he stated clearly. "And I do not trust Ivan."

"Who *do* you trust?"

"That," he said, "is a very good question."

27

When summer arrived and the nights grew shorter, the tempers of those living in the castle began to shrink as well. The warm nights smelled of the roses that grew in the gardens behind the castle; their ripe scent filled the air, and their beauty could not be matched by any other flower in the area. Propped up on a concrete bench, adorned with gargoyle faces on either end, Torenia fingered the pages of the book. Many of the books in the library were children's tales and lore from around the world, others were filled with the history and tactics of war. She had learned much from this single book of the Craft and was beginning to prove her worth.

The most recent tactics meeting had left Torenia feeling superior, not only over everyone in the room, but over Ivan as well. He was the brute—the muscle, the torturer—but Torenia showed that she could handle a situation that threatened the Brotherhood.

Dmitry had returned with demands; if he were to stop the Pure Bloods from attacking, he would need promises. He wished to take Torenia's seat upon the throne—or Ivan's. Demanding that a Pure Blood have his spot on the throne, Dmitry pushed Roman to take action.

"What do you think of this, Ivan?" Roman glanced at his brother. "Your place here is being threatened."

Ivan grinned wildly. "We could take it to The Pits."

"I will not fight you hand to hand." Dmitry scowled, fear dancing in his brown eyes. "But when the army of Pure Bloods comes, I will not stop them."

"Torenia?" Roman suggested. After all, his position was not being threatened, but Torenia's certainly was. She believed Roman would not allow them to be usurped, but he clearly wanted to see how they would handle it. She smiled ever so slightly as she thought of one day taking his throne, a possibility that would have to linger in the back of her mind for a long time before she acted.

Earning Roman's trust and respect was first and foremost.

She rose from her seat, carefully smoothing out her skirts with her black silk gloves. Adorned in the necklace Ivan had given her, a crimson stain on her lips, she otherwise had no color. The black gown, befit for a queen, made her flesh paler than usual; she resembled the queen of death. Everyone watched—including Natasia's daughter, Tasia, who had taken her mother's place after her death—in silence as Torenia walked to where a red-faced Dmitry stood.

Studying him as though he were a cut of meat, she cocked her head to the side. She pursed her lips slightly, walking around him. He spun to follow her, not daring to let her walk behind him. She chuckled lightly at his fear, wondering where this power came from. She reveled in the authority she held just for being part of the Brotherhood. The last time she had been at one of these meetings, she had spoken her piece but remained quite meek throughout it all.

Having seen what Roman was capable of, his ruthlessness when it came to killing Natasia, Torenia had learned. She would no longer allow mercy—not after her mistake with Nikolai—and she had to prove this to Roman. It was clear that this was a test. Nikolai had told her that Roman liked his games.

It was time to play.

Standing before Dmitry, she looked deep into his eyes, her eyelids lowered in a seductive glower. Having learned how Roman killed and the nature in which he conducted himself, Torenia followed suit.

How better to impress than to imitate?

She kissed Dmitry on his paper-skin cheek, leaving a half-lip mark, repeating this on the other side. Looking into his tired, aged eyes, she saw the combination of confusion and lust. He was too confused to know what was coming next and too entranced to breathe. Torenia ran her finger along his jawline, then leaned in to kiss his lips. His tongue was aggressive, finally able to move, and he did not care that everyone in the room was watching, for he was kissing the *Koroleva*. It was a slap in the face to Roman, who demanded equal respect be afforded to her.

Parting from him, Torenia gripped his chin with the tips of her fingers, nails digging into his skin, and grinned wickedly.

"*Koroleva*—" His smug grin turned into a sweep of panic. He clutched his throat, eyes wide, wheezing as the air was unable to pass through. His throat closed, his gagging turning to silence. Moving manically through the room, he knocked over chairs, stumbling into another vampire who jerked out of the way. Dmitry fell to the ground, staring at Torenia as he suffocated.

When silence filled the room, at last, Ivan rose and began to clap.

No one else joined in, everyone staring at Torenia, as she wiped her lower lip with the length of her index finger. She noticed Tasia's lips pulling into the slyest of smiles.

Rouge smudged Torenia's skin as she looked at all the people around her. "My blood status has nothing to do with how I will rule."

Snapping back to the reality around her, Torenia flipped past the pages in the book that told her of poisons and their antidotes. She had applied one to her lips after consuming the antidote, ensuring her safety should she ingest any of it but sure to kill anyone whom she locked lips with. It was a simple potion, one even those who were not witches could concoct, but powerful nonetheless.

Thinking of the future, she decided that, to take what Roman had, she might have to wait until he died. Though this was not her ideal way to usurp him, she had to consider it a possibility. She needed to outlive him and, out of sheer vanity, she wished to remain beautiful when she sat on his throne.

With an eagerness, Torenia opened the book to an unfinished page—virgin blood and the eternal beauty it promised. Unfortunately, whoever penned this theory had never tested it. The other issue was how long it would take to see if it worked. Torenia knew that any other witch who'd gotten her hands on this book would have tested it.

She knew just who to ask.

He appeared like a dog running to a bell, but he was always close when Roman was away.

"Ivan, you are just the person I wished to speak with." Torenia closed the book and stood up. "Walk with me?"

Linking arms with her, he spoke softly. "Should Roman see us…"

"Let him." Torenia waved her hand as if Roman meant nothing. He had been gone for a fortnight to discuss how to proceed with the Pure Blood extremists now that Dmitry was dead, but his return could come at any moment. In the back of her mind, she wondered if he was also seeking her replacement. Rage bubbled deep inside her. "We are walking through the gardens. There is no harm in that, is there?"

Ivan raised a brow and let out a sassy breath of air. "What do you need from me?"

"You're a lover of all things gruesome. Tell me, have you ever heard of bathing in virgin blood to remain youthful?"

"Of course I have." Ivan sounded shocked that Torenia had not. She gestured for him to continue as they entered the labyrinth of hedges. "I've heard rumors of a Countess who bathed in virgin blood."

"For how long? Did she remain youthful?"

"I believe it was two decades; she killed more people than I have," he replied. "So far."

Hedges more than eight feet tall stood all around them, weaving in and out, with entrances and exits all over the place. It was a labyrinth, but one could not get too lost within it. The cold stone below was russet, weeds growing between the cracks, which made the hells of Torenia's shoes clack. The full moon gave the castle a glow; in Torenia's mind, it was the new sun. A full moon, though only three nights a month, was the closest thing she got to sunlight.

She heard a shuffle behind them but pretended she hadn't, for she had an inkling who was following them. An idea popped into her head—something cruel, something that would be the start to some-thing so much more, for she would find eternal beauty, no matter the cost. Ivan was the only person who would understand it, and for that, she was thankful to be in his presence.

"Come closer," she whispered to him.

He stopped quickly and turned to face her, hand on her hip in an instant, the other on her cheek. He paused. "You don't have that... death on your lips, do you?"

She shook her head slowly. "*That* is only for special occasions."

He quickly jerked his head to the side in a shrug and then kissed her deeply. His blue eyes closed, but Torenia's remained open. The figure she was waiting for appeared, her pretty face in sight for only a few seconds before she was gone again. Torenia quickly broke free from Ivan, pushing him on his shoulders. Disappointment crossed his expression until Torenia spoke. "Bring me Irina. Alive."

He grinned, a knowing look in his eyes, before turning on his heel to follow the young maid.

Torenia now knew who had told Roman about her and Ivan.

Torenia also knew whose blood she would bathe in.

28

I van reappeared around the labyrinth hedges with Irina in tow. His hand was wrapped around her bicep, tugging her along with no regard for her cries of pain. She winced when he shoved her to Torenia's feet, her hands reaching out in front of her as she hit the ground. On her hands and knees, Irina collected herself, looking up at Torenia. Tears welled in the corners of her eyes.

"Spying for Roman? Or your own guilty pleasure?" Torenia asked sharply.

Irina leaned back, sitting on her calves. She wiped tears from her eyes before they fell, meeting Torenia's blue stare. She whispered shakily, "I simply stumbled upon you, that is all, *Koroleva*."

"That is highly unlikely." Torenia glanced at Ivan, who was standing behind Irina. "What do you think, Ivan?"

"Do you want her dead or alive?" he asked.

Irina began to beg, "Please, *Koroleva*, please! I was not spying, I promise! Please, I beg you, I will do anything!"

"Alive, Ivan. Irina knows better than anyone that I like my bath hot."

Irina began to shout for help, crawling away from Ivan, but not fast enough. He grabbed her by her dress collar and yanked her back so hard she choked, her eyes bugging out. Irina kicked and clawed as

Ivan pulled her along behind Torenia, no doubt watching the smooth way her hips swayed as she walked out of the labyrinth toward the doors that led inside the castle.

By the time they arrived at Torenia's bedroom, Irina's face was tear-streaked and she was crying so violently that she shook. Torenia opened the bathroom door and lit the lamps. She drew the curtains back so that the moonlight could pour in, basking in it for a moment before she turned back to face them. Removing her lace gloves, she draped them over the back of the vanity chair where she had sat so many times while Irina stood behind her, brushing her long black hair.

She was a good maid, but Torenia didn't need people to wait on her. Especially if they were reporting to Roman.

Torenia crouched in front of Irina, tilting her chin up so that they could look each other in the eyes when they spoke, woman to woman. "Tell me, Irina, what ran through your pretty little head when you saw Ivan and me in the library? Hmm? Have you ever seen a man's hand caress a woman's thigh? Has anyone ever laid with you?"

Despite the position she was in, Irina blushed. "No, *Koroleva*."

"Excellent." Torenia released her, then began to disrobe garment by garment. She walked towards the bathroom and turned to beckon Ivan and Irina closer.

Ivan dragged Irina over to the tub, holding her over the porcelain. From his inner jacket pocket, he withdrew a small blade. Though Torenia knew he preferred hands-on killing—there were an unlimited number of tools that could make it all much more exciting. One glance at Torenia, shamelessly caressing her with his eyes, he waited for her command. When she nodded, he slowly slit Irina's throat. The girl's eyes went wide, her hands releasing her grip on the edge of the tub and going to her throat as she desperately attempted to close the wound. Blood gushed from her like a waterfall, filling the bottom of the basin with deep, rich crimson color. Irina wept as the life drained out of her.

Torenia looked into the tub after Ivan had drained all he could from Irina. She pouted. "Well, this will not do. How many maids are there here? How old are they, usually?"

"Maybe a dozen." Ivan was amazed by her sadism. The hungry look in his eyes told Torenia that she had him right where she wanted him. "I cannot tell you which ones are virgins, though I could tell you which ones aren't."

Torenia smirked. "Bring me all whom you have not bedded, please."

"Yes, *Koroleva*."

"And Ivan." She turned to face him as he walked through the doorway. He paused to look at her. "Make it quick. I don't want the blood to go cold."

Within the hour, Torenia was soaking in the thick, crimson liquid. Leaning back against the tub, she reveled in it, wondering how on earth it had taken her so long to discover it. Her skin soaked it in; she felt refreshed and replenished as the blood began to grow cold. In her hand was a crystal wine glass filled with blood from the youngest maid; she had been naught but twelve. Bathing in all that youth, it was bound to do what she believed it would.

She wondered about the possibilities; if she could stay young, could she bring back the dead? She would become the world's most powerful witch if she could accomplish that.

Heavy footsteps coming through her bedroom startled her, but she remained composed and relaxed as Roman burst through the bathroom door. "I am gone a fortnight and every single maid is dead?"

"Not all of them," Torenia retorted.

"You killed Irina." She knew he did not show concern for the girl, but for the information she had been feeding him.

"I found her gallivanting when she should have been working, her usefulness had run out."

Roman's jaw shifted, then set. "You do not get to decide that, she was my—"

"Your spy?" Torenia finished for him. "I understand you wanted to keep an eye on me when I first arrived, but I have been here for some time now. If I am to be your equal, I will not have you watching my every move. From now on, I will select my maids, and they will not be your eyes and ears."

"Torenia, you are taking this too far," Roman declared. "An equal you are, yes. But do not think for a moment that you are a *Brother.*"

"I do not wish to be," she snarled, knowing that he meant, despite having equal status, she would not have equal power unless she made it happen. "Tell me, did the Pure Bloods attack after I killed Dmitry? You went to meet with them, did you not? You appear unharmed."

A muscle in his jaw twitched, and she knew she had won. He cracked his neck, then sighed. "They were quite compliant."

She smiled briefly. "You are very welcome, Roman."

Before he could say anything more, she drained the last of the blood in the crystal glass and then stood up in the tub. The quickest way to get Roman to leave her alone was to make him uncomfortable. Though he acted as if nothing truly bothered him, Roman would quickly navigate away when she flaunted herself like this. Her pale flesh was covered from chest to toe in blood. It dripped off her body and pooled on the floor.

"Would you be so kind as to hand me a towel?" she asked.

Roman grabbed the stark white towel and watched as Torenia draped it around her frame. When she was covered, he cleared his throat. "A new leader for the Pure Blooded has been appointed."

"Who?" Her blood ran cold; the only reason Roman would mention this would be to remind her that her position was feeble. She had nothing to do with Pure Blood affairs, but the threat still hung over her. Perhaps now had been the wrong time to act out against Roman. After all, she was on thin ice to begin with since she lost Nikolai.

"Someone very dear to me."

29

Torenia bathed—though not in blood this night, merely scalding hot water, oils, and rose petals. Her finger made tiny whirlpools with lazy movements. To her left, the last maid in the house remained. She was younger than Torenia, though boring in appearance. After she had drawn Torenia's bath, Torenia gave her a little tonic to make her drowsy and numb. Then, she hooked a small needle and tube to her throat, letting the blood fill the chalice at the end of it.

Bringing the chalice to her lips, Torenia drank the fresh, youthful blood. Roman had left not long after his return. To fetch her replacement, she feared. But she would not give up her position so easily. She had made enough of an impact at each tactics meeting that her removal from the Brotherhood, or her death, would not go unnoticed and unchallenged.

With Roman gone, she relaxed in the way she knew best, dealing with each obstacle he placed before her. Every maid in the castle would be cleared out by the end of the night to make way for the new batch she was bringing in. Instead of being in Roman's employ, they would be hers. If Roman had gone out of his way to find someone who was going to possibly replace her, she would have infiltrated her castle with her own little birds.

She ruminated fondly on her memories of Madam Scarlett.

A knock came on the bathroom door, and Torenia sighed. Was no place sacred?

"Come in," she called, not bothering to hide the frustration from her voice.

A tall, muscular figure she had grown to recognize with ease entered.

"Oh, Ivan." Her voice carried the essence of relief.

A small, yet ever so noticeable, shudder vibrated through Ivan. His blue eyes were wide and, as always, hungry. "The things I would do for you to say that one more time."

"Oh..." She paused and watched his reaction. The way Ivan stirred at her drawn-out word. A sound with so much meaning. "Do tell me."

He grinned, glancing at the docile maid seated next to the bath. "Is she the last one?"

"For now."

"Roman is away," he told her, eyes traveling back to Torenia to watch her expression.

Torenia decided to have a little fun. Roman had explicitly told her to stay away from Ivan and, he had most certainly told Ivan to stay far away from her. Yet here he was, crawling like a dog back to his true master when he was gone. Who was Roman to say who she was permitted to play with?

"Take off your coat."

Ivan didn't hesitate, slipping it off of his broad frame. He reached for the hem of his shirt, then saw the stern look on Torenia's face and stopped. His hands trembled ever so slightly as he did so, before bringing them to his sides and awaiting her next command.

"And your shirt," she said, sounding bored. She sipped her blood, not even watching him as he removed his shirt. When she casually glanced back, she was unsurprised, but still wildly turned on at the sight of his scarred body. Half of him was covered in tattoos, the other half scars from years of fights and wars. She thought briefly of when she first saw him, fighting a bear like a maniac.

"Kneel beside her." As he did this, she placed the chalice on the ground and leaned over the side of the basin. Detaching the needle from the maid's neck, she let it fall to the floor. Blood splattered along the tiles.

"Feed," she commanded. "Slowly."

Ivan's eyes flickered to her, then back to the woman beside him. With tender hands, he tilted her head back and lapped up the blood that dribbled down her neck where the needle had been. Once it was spotless, he bit down with a moan.

Torenia watched, her hand disappearing beneath the water. Ivan kept his eyes on Torenia as he slowly devoured. The slowness was nearly impossible for a vampire, but Ivan proved his determination to please Torenia.

In response, Torenia leaned back against the tub's rim, letting her hair fall over the edge, water sloshing over the sides as she pleasured herself. She watched Ivan's eyelids flutter, but he never shut them, as if waiting for her. The moment she reached her crescendo, she forced a single word out. "Stop".

Ivan stopped with a groan, releasing his hold on the maid who hardly had any life left in her.

"Give," she said, wondering what Ivan would do with this command. He pushed the maid aside, the only obstacle between him and Torenia, and got inside the tub. Torenia expected him to have removed his trousers, but instead, he cupped either side of her head and brought his mouth to hers. A wave of blood filled her mouth.

When Ivan released her, his voice was husky. "I will give, and give, and give."

"Oh..." she said with a grin, watching his anticipation build. "Ivan."

Torenia left Ivan wanting so that she could attend to her duties—she had a staff to hire, one that would not be under Roman's influence. She had the throne room to herself, and the antechamber was filled with a group of young women from across the country who sought employment. Torenia offered protection, shelter, food, and wages to them or to be sent to their families if they had left those behind. All she asked was that they were loyal to only her.

One by one, they scurried in to tell their stories to beg for Torenia to take them in—after all, the position was prestigious and sought after. There was competition, for she only wanted half a dozen. Roman could hire more staff if he wanted—people to clean and take care of the grounds—but Torenia would not let anyone within her room to tend to her needs unless she approved of them.

Most were thin and desperate. The journey to the Brotherhood was perilous, and one woman spoke of her friend who had died on the way. Torenia's heart didn't ache for the deceased she did not know. As they filtered through, she quickly dismissed the ones she did not trust—too meek, too terrified. They would crack under Roman's gaze in an instant.

She needed someone hardened.

As the pickings grew slim and, having only selected three that would be able to carry out trivial tasks such as drawing her bath and bringing her blood to dine on, the final woman entered. The doors from the antechamber opened wide and in came a woman so striking that Torenia couldn't take her eyes off her. She was young, but with a depth in her gray eyes that sparked with a lingering ember of rage.

"*Koroleva*," the woman greeted, kneeling with fluidity. When Torenia nodded, the woman rose. Her cheeks were full and red, kissed by the mountain air. "I am Anja."

"And why have you come here, Anja?" Torenia managed to ask, keeping her voice steady enough, but wondering if Anja could hear its gentle tremor.

"I've heard of the woman who earned her spot on the Brotherhood and thought there would be no better place for me," Anja replied. Her hands were clasped in front of her voluptuous hips. She was muscular, Torenia could tell that even under the layers of heavy clothing.

"This is a position for an attendee to my needs, nothing more," Torenia reminded Anja, who seemed too strong for a position like this. "Why would you want to work for me, specifically?"

"I am aware of the position, *Koroleva*. I am happy to provide you with anything you need." She smiled slightly. "I am tired of working for men who do not respect me. I want to work for a woman who will fight for me."

Torenia's eyes lit up, her cheeks aglow. "And fight for you I will, you have my promise. I like you, Anja."

"You do not know me, *Koroleva*."

"I would like to know you," Torenia admitted, surprising herself and Anja. She cleared her throat, getting back to the task at hand. "You know the cost of being in my employ?"

"Yes." Anja nodded, never taking her eyes off Torenia. The others had shuddered in her presence, unable to maintain eye contact, yet Anja was devouring Torenia, hungry for her in a way Ivan never could understand.

"To pledge your loyalty to me I ask for little," Torenia said to the few bold faces before her. Anja stood with her hands behind her back, casually clasped. The others trembled ever so slightly, hardly noticeable to the human eye. However, Torenia's senses were keen, and she could feel their pulses increase.

"Three marks upon your flesh, done only with your consent," she continued. "One mark on mine. We will be tethered, though you may leave my employ at any time. Our tether will not bind us in any way save for your loyalty to me and my protection of you. No harm will come to any of you under this roof.

"I ask that what you learn in my presence remain unspoken. Most of you will be tending to fairly simple needs. Washing the linens, tidying my space, drawing my baths, running my errands." Torenia glanced between the women before her. "Should you desire anything, you need only ask."

She unwrapped a blade with a bone handle, curved ever so slightly. It gleamed in the lantern light. "Shall we begin?"

They all nodded or spoke their assent, and Torenia removed the robe she wore. The shift she wore underneath was low at the back, revealing her spine. She handed the first maid, Katerina, the blade and turned her back on them. Though she trusted few, she had to be vulnerable for this cast to succeed. The piercing feeling over the vertebrae and between her shoulder blades made her hiss, the slow trickle of blood tickling her spine.

Katerina's thumb caught the trail of blood, and Torenia turned to face her. The servant's blonde hair hung loose and simple as she smeared the blood over each of Torenia's cheeks, following one line down her forehead. She then placed the blade into Torenia's hand.

Exactly where the blood was smeared on her own face, Torenia carved those same marks into Katerina's. She felt the pain Katerina did, though she would have no scars to show for it save for the one on her spine.

"*Facti sumus unum per sanguinem.*"

The blood magic pulsed in the air around them like a heartbeat. The cast continued with each maid Torenia bound to her, a new scar down her back for each woman, resembling a ladder. Anja went last. Her hands were strong yet gentle as she spread Torenia's shoulder blades, nestling the dagger in between them. Torenia felt her breath upon her marred skin and shuddered, Anja making a soft sound when Torenia's skin rippled under her palm.

Her skin split. More blood was spilled—the room reeked of it. With each initiation the power of the magic was stronger. Each movement of Anja's was performed with the utmost care; the way her thumb ran over each previous wound, then stopped at the cut she had just made. The magic pulsed faster, beating with the rapidity of Torenia's own heart as she turned to face Anja.

Anja never blinked as she spread Torenia's blood across her already-stained cheeks and forehead. She smiled crookedly when Torenia brought the blade to her face. As though there was no one else in the room, they were cocooned within the blood magic, protected by it before the casting was completed.

"Go ahead," Anja whispered. "Bind me to you."

Torenia marveled at Anja's stoic face as she made the cuts. "*Facti sumus unum per sanguinem.*"

"We become one through blood," Anja echoed.

30

Torenia thought long and hard about who Roman would try to replace her with; who was dear to a man with no concept of emotion? It had been two months since he had announced the existence of this mysterious person, and neither Torenia nor Ivan had an inkling of who it could possibly be. They were to be revealed at that evening's meeting.

The Pure Bloods had recently backed off; the rogue parties who refused to be under the control of only Half Blood vampires still lingered but, without support due to Dmitry's death, they had receded for the time being. It was time to take full control of the situation; they were weak and scared. Torenia had learned a lot from ruling alongside Roman and Ivan but equally learned a lot from herself.

She had learned not to trust anyone, not even the new maids she had selected. Her maids, unlike Roman's, were vampires. Marked with scars on their foreheads and cheeks, the purple markings were all hollow. Every maid she took in was beautiful, with a certain grace that was only seen in those who held their heads high. Despite the fact that she had scarred them permanently to diminish their beauty, they all had utmost loyalty to her; each maid had accepted these scars willingly. She trusted them enough, but she knew that Roman had a way with words and was very convincing when he set his mind to something.

There was only one she trusted fully.

"Anja," Torenia called as she got out of the tub. She now bathed in blood once a week, but today it was only steaming hot waters that scalded her replenished skin.

"Yes, *Koroleva*?" Anja's round face was filled with youthful beauty; she was barely older than twenty but was both wise and resourceful.

"If your position was being threatened, what would you do?" Torenia knew that the meeting that night would be one that could easily change her life. If Roman had someone he planned to take over Dmitry's position, when it was Torenia who had taken out Dmitry, she no longer trusted that Roman would give her the respect she deserved. She would have to take what he had.

Anja smirked. "I've learned a lot from being the lowest on the food chain—"

"Not the lowest. Men are below us."

"I mean being a woman."

Torenia's expression hardened, for she understood.

"People think we are weak, that we can do no harm, and so they are careless around us. A slip of the tongue, mindless banter—I listen to all of it. I see all angles, the list of possible reasons someone does something. Listening is the most important skill and, when you have listened enough, you strike."

"Who wronged you?" Torenia asked as she flipped through her gowns, trying to select one that was not too modest but still mature.

"I worked for someone else before I was turned; he took quite a liking to me," Anja explained as she pulled out a gown she thought would suit Torenia. It was long, solid black, with a slit along the left leg. The bust had a sweetheart neckline that put her pale skin and curves on display. As Torenia took her advice for her attire, Anja continued. "I listened one night as he spoke with a friend about an important deal he had to make; if it did not go through, he would not survive as a family man. His wife was pregnant—she ended up having twins—and he needed to secure his finances. He was going to sell a piece of land, enough to keep him financially stable.

"That night, I snuck into his office after he'd fallen asleep." She spoke the words so sharply that Torenia knew what he'd done before he had fallen asleep. "I found the paper that proved his rights to the land. I then went to his wife and gave her the paper, so that she knew the land existed, and I told her what was happening, what her husband was doing to me; she was enraged, and I watched as she murdered him with a kitchen knife.

"She sold that land, had her twins, and, from what I have heard, is doing quite well. See, I did nothing that would have gotten me incarcerated or worse. I waited and listened until I had what I needed. The deed to the property made her trust me when I told her about the rape, and she did everything else herself. I earned her trust, I made alliances, and then I was able to use her to carry out my deeds."

"Thank you for your honesty, Anja." Torenia pondered this, wondering how she could use it to her advantage.

"For you, *Koroleva*, anything." Anja bowed her head.

Torenia placed her hand under Anja's chin and lifted her head. Looking into her rich gray eyes, she spoke softly to the other woman. "You need not ever bow to me."

Torenia stood outside Roman's office, a room in the castle that she had never entered before. A place of power, a room she was barred from. She raised her hand to knock on the door, wanting to inquire as to whether she would be humiliated at the meeting. At least if she knew she was going to be replaced, she could prepare herself for it. A sweet scent emitted from the room, so Torenia knew Roman was in there.

Hushed voices could be heard when she listened closely.

Finally, Torenia knocked.

"Not now," Roman's voice thundered through the door.

Torenia opened her mouth to speak, then shut it. Rage billowed up, filling her entire body. She turned on her heel, walking slowly to allow her fury to diminish. The meeting room was not far from Roman's office; though she was early, she entered.

In the great meeting room, where a roaring fire in the center of the far wall brought too much heat for her comfort, Torenia took her seat. Earlier than usual, she was not surprised to find the room empty. Her worry made her palms sweat, so she placed her hands on her thighs. The room began to fill up with the faces of people she had grown accustomed to seeing once every few months.

There was Viktor, a Half Blood who was married to Arina, a Pure Blood. Together, they were a prime example of perfection; neither cared about the other's status, they were content with who ran the Brotherhood, and their input was always well received. Yulia was a high-status Pure Blood who rarely spoke; instead, she listened and never caused trouble. She had been excellent at keeping the rebellious Pure Bloods in her city on a leash. Most of them followed her like dogs, and Torenia envied her. Pyotr and Vasily came from further North, and they brought with them dozens of Half Blood fighters to defend the Brotherhood and surrounding areas from any attacks.

When everyone was seated, Ivan walked in and slumped down in the seat between Roman and Torenia. Normally he sat across from her, but this spot had clearly been left open for Roman's guest. Ivan eyed her cautiously, then directed his attention to the voices coming down the hall. Everyone waited in silence as Roman neared. Entering, he surveyed the crowd and, with a nod of acceptance, gestured for his mystery guest to come in.

There was no other way to describe her—she was gorgeous. The word barely held a candle to her. With shoulder-length, jet-black hair that was pinned back simply, her face was on full display. Her pale cheeks were round, subtle youthfulness hiding there. With the same striking blue eyes that Roman, Ivan, and Nikolai possessed, there was no doubt in Torenia's mind that she was related to them in some way.

"Brothers and Sisters, this is my daughter, Svetlana," he introduced.

Torenia leaned over and whispered to Ivan. "I thought he had no interest in women."

"He wanted an heir," Ivan replied, though he did not take his eyes off Roman and Svetlana.

"You knew?"

"Of course."

"Why didn't you tell me?" Torenia hissed.

"I did not think it was important."

"Not important?" She wanted to smack him. "Two months of trying to find out who would be important to him, and you did not think to mention he had a daughter?"

Ivan shrugged. "I have not seen her since her birth. She's quite...*exquisite.*"

Torenia scowled; she did not need to have it pointed out that she was gorgeous, prettier than Torenia. An ancient feeling bubbled up inside of her, something she had not felt since she last saw Aster—spiteful jealousy. When Svetlana took her seat where Ivan normally sat, her blue eyes met with Torenia's. She reeked of innocence, untouched by the cruelty of the Brotherhood and the wars that surrounded it. She was inept at warfare, but Torenia had been once, too.

"If she wasn't my niece..." Ivan smirked.

Torenia chose to ignore that comment. "Is she Pure Blood?"

"Of course, her mother is an Old Blood. Roman had to have a backup, should Nikolai truly disappear. We anticipated his weakness back when he was a child."

Torenia's position was threatened, hanging in the balance.

She knew exactly what she had to do.

Even her voice was melodic.

When the meeting concluded, everyone rose from their seats. No small talk ever occurred after these meetings, everyone dispersing until the next time they gathered. Only the four of them remained. Roman stood beside his daughter, who was tall and slender, her large blue eyes with hints of gray; not menacing like Ivan and Roman's, but soft and curious.

"Torenia, it is good to meet you." Svetlana broke the silence first.

Torenia held out her hand to shake Svetlana's. "Likewise, Svetlana. I was unaware Roman had a daughter."

"Please, call me Lana," she offered, speaking as though they were going to become great friends. "Father wished I remained away from all of this to keep me safe."

"And yet here you are," Torenia sang, her voice dripping with venom.

"And Uncle Ivan." Lana embraced Ivan, who stood shocked and did not hug back. "I have only heard about you, like a storybook character!"

"More like a horror story," Torenia mumbled. Ivan glanced at her throughout the deeply uncomfortable hug, his eyebrow raised sharply. But he was not offended by Torenia's words, for both of them knew that the things they loved and craved were things of nightmares, not childish tales.

Lana broke from Ivan, who stepped back awkwardly, and then left the room swiftly. Roman remained like an overseer of the two women meeting. Lana was very hands-on, taking Torenia's forearms in her warm hands, clutching them as sisters might. Everything she did made her appear so young, and naïve to what really happened within these walls. Torenia wondered if she knew about the harvest; surely she did. She was a Pure Blood and would know Man as nothing more than food. It would not keep her up at night, as it might for a vampire who turned later in life.

"I have heard so much about you," Lana said. "You're a beacon to us all. I wish only to be half as powerful as you, Torenia."

Torenia raised a sharp eyebrow. "Do you study the Craft?"

"Only the basics. I would not call myself an avid student. I could certainly never hold a candle to you."

Torenia took this piece of information and stored it, deciding she had to treat Lana like someone she actually liked. She had to pretend to care about her, to teach her, to take her under her wing, and make her trust her. To have Lana close would be to her utmost advantage. Anja's advice was already proving useful.

"Perhaps you should ask your father if I can teach you more," Torenia suggested, turning to look at Roman and gauge his reaction.

"Teachings will be every evening," he declared, clearly having already decided this. He wanted Torenia to expend her time and resources training her own replacement. "First thing."

"We will begin tomorrow." Torenia nodded in agreement. The more she tried to remain one step ahead, the more she realized Roman was already two steps past her. She needed him to distrust his daughter enough to send her away.

Autumn hit that week, the leaves suddenly relinquishing their hold on the branches they had clung to for months and drifting in a see-saw motion to the ground. The onslaught of leaves covered the grounds around the castle, sprinkling it with brilliant oranges and browns, yellows and reds. The days were growing shorter, the nights longer. Evening came earlier every day, giving them more time to study and learn. Though Torenia had learned a lot in the last few months of focusing on her studies, she still discovered more every day, especially when she began to teach Lana.

They were in the library with the curtains drawn back so the moonlight could flood the space with light. The smell of the old books surrounded them. They had only been studying together for a few days, but Lana looked at Torenia daily with wide eyes, eager to learn. Torenia wondered if she had looked like that when she approached Madam Scarlett all those years ago.

"Your father," Torenia began, "did he visit you often?"

She nodded. "Oh yes, weekly when I was a child, less so when the war was ongoing. After Nikolai left, he grew too busy."

"And your mother? Ivan mentioned she was...Old Blood?"

"A strict woman, the studying she made me do was far less pleasant than it is with you." She smiled at Torenia, her big eyes seeking acceptance. "She says we are Old Blood; her family has always been vampire, for as long as the records go back."

She had not heard the term and wondered why they were not a problem to the Brotherhood.

"I know what you're thinking, but you don't need to fear the Old Bloods. They are often a sickly group. I do not like to admit it, but many have been somewhat inbred. Because of my vitality," she paused and Torenia soaked in her youth, "I do not believe my mother is actually Old Blood, but lied for status."

Torenia smiled back, so sweetly that it made her cheeks ache, but she had to win over Lana; she had to use the young, naïve girl to her advantage. If she was the only person who meant anything to Roman, then the best thing she could do was make Lana choose her over her father.

She changed the topic. "And what did she make you study so thoroughly?"

"Pure Blooded history." Her face fell. "It was very...disturbing. Did you know that Half Bloods were created to see if vampires could survive the sunlight? And when they could not survive it, just like Pure Bloods, they were considered half-breeds, lesser than Pure Bloods. Pure Bloods sought the extinction of Half Bloods."

"Well..." Torenia thought about her words carefully, "you cannot have just any Pure Blood on the throne. One must be very well-versed in what they are ruling and understand the welfare of Half Bloods."

"Ruling? Oh, no, Torenia, I simply keep the peace among the Pure Blooded. A seat upon the throne beside my father, Ivan, and you..." She shook her head. "I would never dream of it."

This surprised Torenia. Reaching over, she held Lana's smooth hands in her own. "You must dream bigger, Lana. Why do you think Roman created you? Why do you think he insisted you be well-versed in Pure Blood history? He wishes you to take his spot when he is gone. But why should you wait?"

Lana pulled her hands back. "Torenia, I will not usurp my father."

"Of course not, but do not let yourself become his stepping-stone to controlling the Pure Blooded. You are so much more than that, Lana. A woman of your kindness and benevolence, you could rule in a way Roman never could. It is time the Brotherhood starts considering a new angle. A Sisterhood, perhaps."

"You mean to say..." Lana nibbled her lip nervously, then looked back at Torenia. "You think that I could stop the fighting?"

"Not when you sit around the table, only if you sit upon the throne." Torenia planted the seed in her mind. Despite being

Roman's daughter, she was nothing like him. She marveled at the flowers and birds that perched in the windows. She smiled frequently and followed Torenia around like a duckling. But Torenia had to remind herself that she *was* Roman's daughter; she could be playing a far more dangerous game than Torenia knew. She had to remain one step ahead.

"Don't be a pawn when you should be a Queen—the most powerful piece on the board."

31

Torenia walked the halls of the castle, peering up at the paintings of previous battles. Battles led by bloodthirsty males who fought ruthlessly, without tact. Each gilded frame held another depiction of war: piles of bodies, heads on spikes, vampire armies with teeth bared. As she progressed to another wing of the castle, she saw that all the doors had been left open, save for one—Roman's study.

The place where he pondered his battles, plotting his next steps to save what was clearly a dying regime. He was hanging on by a thread, trying to keep his pawns alive, not realizing he had already lost his Queen and that she was going to take him down with his knight and bishop. She walked by the study without slowing.

She continued to the library, where she found Svetlana. The girl was poring over a book and, when Torenia got close, she noticed it was a play. Some fiction about star-crossed lovers. Sometimes it was unbelievable that she was Roman's daughter—she made it too easy for Torenia to manipulate her. In nearly a year, Torenia had molded Svetlana into everything Roman hated.

"Lana." Torenia's voice was stern, causing the younger woman to jump. Careless, unaware, and less like Roman than he wanted her to be. "Should you not be preparing for this season's meeting?"

"He exhausts me, Torenia," Lana replied. "He never listens to what I say. What I bring to the table is valuable, and he refuses to see it."

"Some men wear blinders." Torenia saw Svetlana's eyes widen as her lips parted. "However...this makes them blind in many areas."

"Is it time?" Lana asked.

"Are you ready?" Torenia walked over to where a candle sat with a flickering flame. She turned her back to Svetlana as she waved her hand over the flame, feeling it gently burn her. "To do what needs to be done?"

"Yes."

Torenia snuffed out the flame.

"The remaining Pure Blood outliers will be executed. Publicly. End of discussion," Roman told those gathered around the table. Torenia still sat beside him, Ivan opposite her. The regular faces, whom Torenia was growing more comfortable around, were nodding. Men were being kept in check, Pure Bloods were no longer revolting, and even the smaller groups that were more stubborn and extreme were losing ground. After a few public executions, there would be very few left to rally any sort of retaliation.

"Actually, I would like to suggest some changes," Svetlana said, standing. All eyes were on her, but Torenia glanced down the table to study the others. Tasia, her hair soft and blonde like her mother's but without the subtle gray hairs, was watching Torenia, not Svetlana. She gave Torenia a gentle nod, then turned her gaze to Svetlana.

She wondered what that nod meant—did she see what Torenia was doing and agree with it? No, she decided; it was more likely that Tasia saw that Torenia was helping women at this table to have a voice. Tasia was someone Torenia wanted to speak with but had never been given the opportunity. She was someone who understood power but also understood when to stay away. She never spoke of Roman murdering her mother, and Torenia wondered if she knew the truth and was biding her time.

"I do not think that rounding up the leaders of those outlying groups and having them killed is going to solve the problem," Svetlana argued.

"The discussion is over," Roman declared. "You're a child, Svetlana, you do not understand the ugliness of war."

"There is no war!" she shouted. "You are going to create one if you keep slaughtering those who oppose you."

"Sit. Down." Roman got to his feet, towering over his daughter.

"We need to offer them something," she said, no fear in how she spoke to her father now. Torenia had told her to act like a queen instead of a pawn, but she hadn't told her how to do it with tact. Lana was doing everything wrong, exactly how Torenia had planned.

"I offer them the chance to acquiesce and live, or revolt and die," Roman snapped. "This discussion is over."

Everyone understood, rising in an uncomfortable shuffle, ignoring Roman and Svetlana's heated standoff. As everyone filed out, Roman grabbed Svetlana's arm and guided her out of the room. Torenia took this moment to approach Tasia without Roman being around to listen.

"May I ask what that was about?" Torenia asked, linking arms with Tasia.

The young blonde smiled. "The girl is right—we need to start making some changes. Particularly in the leadership of our kind."

"Are you suggesting—"

"I am merely planting the seed," Tasia cut her off. "Women need their voices to be heard. And no one takes our voices seriously when we are under a male."

"You could not be more right," Torenia agreed.

"In time, I suspect I will be answering to you." They paused, now completely alone. No one lurked here; it was silent.

"No," Torenia shook her head. "Don't think for one second I've forgotten what Roman did to your mother."

Tasia's lips pressed together tightly. "Nor I."

"I believe the lot of them will be answering to us."

"Us," Tasia said, tasting it. Then she nodded. "Oh, how I like the sound of that."

"I must be going, but consider the seed planted."

Torenia stood in the hallway out of sight, listening to Roman and Lana shouting at one another in his study. The seed she had planted in Lana's head so long ago was finally blooming. The young vampire wanted power—more than her father, more than Ivan. Svetlana believed that, with her father's power, she could bring about the peace he never could.

Hiding behind the corner, the doors to Roman's study reflecting in the window, Torenia listened intently. Eagerness consumed her, for she had waited a very long time for this moment. The moment that Roman would see through his daughter's desperation for power, when he would finally push her away, after realizing she only wished to have more than him, to take it from him.

Torenia watched the reflection in the window as the doors flew open, and Lana stormed out, Roman's heavy steps seconds behind her. He pointed a gruesome finger, the nail black and threatening. His voice did not shake, but his anger was evident. "Do not walk away from me, Svetlana!"

She turned on her heel to address her father. "I've been here for *months,* and you have given me *nothing!*"

"Nothing?" He stepped into her personal space, towering above her. "Safety, protection, an endless food supply, anything you could ever ask for—"

"Except a spot on the throne, I have to wait until you die for that," she hissed, jabbing her finger into Roman's chest.

He grabbed her hand and shoved it aside, ignoring her wince. "You so desperately want my role, but you do not understand the weight that comes with it. You are not made for leading; you are weak, you are *kind.* The Brotherhood does not need women who pity the weak, it needs strength, Svetlana, and you are not what I hoped you would be."

"And *what* did you hope for from me?" Her voice was broken.

"I wished for you to be ruthless," he said, "like Torenia."

Torenia felt her heart leap into her throat; everything was going far better than she had expected. To be seen as the superior Sister, to have Lana sent away, for Roman to distrust her because of her desperate need for power. A grin crept upon her face as she strained to hear what else Roman had to say about her.

"You dabble in witchcraft but make no headway. You know about Pure Bloods; you frown upon their ruthlessness, but you do nothing to stop it. You do not understand war. If I allowed you to sit upon the throne, you'd let it crumble. You'd let them walk all over us; I need a Pure Blood on the throne, but I would rather let Nikolai take over than see you there."

Lana let out a sob, choking it back the best she could. "Father, please..."

"Go back to your mother," Roman finished, slamming the door.

Torenia waited until Lana had left, packing her bags before a chaperone took her back to her mother's home. Only then did she approach Roman, pretending to be unaware of the events that had occurred and that her only knowledge was that Lana had left. She knocked tentatively on the door to his study.

"Enter," he called, stress lining his voice.

She entered the study, feeling its presence cocoon the essence of Roman within. A wall of shelves lined with books greeted her, framing a hearth with a fire burning gently within. Atop the hearth was a stick of incense, burning a woody, pine smell. A large wooden desk that was void of anything upon it—save for a little blue book—stood between her and Roman.

"Brother," she spoke softly, with a slight concern that was entirely false. "Why have you sent Lana away?"

He glared at her, trying to read through her words, torn between trust and distrust. "She grovels for power like a mutt."

"It has been many months; does she not deserve some title, some power?" Torenia posed, though the words were meant for her own hard work put into this Brotherhood. It was hanging together by threads, and Roman's power was beginning to dwindle. She would have to make her move soon, now.

"No, Torenia; she had not earned it."

"What must she do to earn it?" Torenia asked, her gaze slipping momentarily to the little blue book. A book of lore, she gauged, from the worn-down remains of the title. What a strange thing for Roman to have.

Roman glanced up at her, rising from his seat and placing his fingers on the desk. His fingers bent, white at the knuckles. "Are you asking for her, or for yourself?"

"I am appreciative of what you have given me. Man does not revolt because I have made sure of that," she replied. "I do not want *more,* I want to *do* more."

"I see right through you, Torenia, do not think you have put on a façade that is impenetrable."

"I am not asking for power. I have already accomplished much on my own—you cannot deny that," she said. "I am asking what you want me to do to be worthy of it. You wanted a witch and a queen. You got one. So why hold her back?"

"Find me Nikolai," he responded, without missing a beat.

Alone in the library, the very place Torenia had learned everything she could so far, she felt comfort consume her. This was her place and now that Lana was out of the way, it was her own again. With a quill and ink, she penned in the ancient book bound in human flesh, the Witch Testament, as she'd begun to call it. She had been using it to write down her learning and discoveries as all the others before her had so those who came after her could follow her guide. There had been pages torn out, Torenia noticed over the years, and she had lost sleep over what those lost pages might contain.

What she needed now was to channel the voice that sometimes spoke to her. She needed guidance and knew she needed to alter her mental state to bring the voice forward. Torenia suspected it would be somewhat like bonding with Rahella. So she scoured those pages until she found a potion for enhanced susceptibility to bonding.

In a small pot hanging over the great fire that lit the library, Torenia carefully measured out ingredients. She did not need much, the odd herb and liquid to make the potion bubble and brew. The most important ingredient was to come from her own body, so she withdrew a dagger and spread her fingers, palm up. Slicing the flesh open, she watched the blood bubble up from the wound, then clutched her fingers into a fist, draining it out over the pot. The potion bubbled viciously, rattling the little pot, before dwindling to a simmer.

After brewing for a few minutes, Torenia removed the pot and let it cool before pouring it into a goblet. A soft click against the window told her that Rahella was there, ever a comforting presence. The bird eyed Torenia knowingly, for they shared their thoughts at all times, their connection unbreakable.

"Unbreakable…" Torenia muttered to herself, her mind wandering, before drinking back the vile potion. It burned her tongue and throat but warmed her belly like a spirit. With her eyes closed, she inhaled deeply and spoke. "Are you there?"

"*Yes.*"

"Where?"

"*Where the balance has been tipped.*" The voice was clearer than ever before. "*And the waters run black.*"

"This is where I can find you?"

"*Yes and no.*"

"Is this where I will find Nikolai Sokolov?"

"*Yes.*"

"Who are you?"

"*The Seer.*"

"What is your name?"

But the voice did not reply.

32

The threat of failure hung over her, but Torenia refused to succumb to it. The task Roman had handed her was daunting, but she had the Seer on her side. At least, she hoped that the Seer was on her side. For now, she had to trust that she was.

Torenia rang a bell to summon Anja and began to scour the shelves of the library while she waited for her to arrive. She had gathered a hefty stack of seven books by the time Anja arrived. She stood in the doorway, one hand in the frame, the other hanging loosely at her side. She wore a dress that wrapped around her, leaving parts of her skin exposed.

"You called?" Anja asked casually. They had overcome the need to address one another as queen and servant; they were more than that. She had been more than that the moment she had entered the castle.

Torenia forgot momentarily what she had called Anja for and stepped towards her. Sliding her hand on either side of her hips, she pulled Anja close. Anja lifted her head and let her lips hover just before Torenia's. She smelled like honey and lavender, calming Torenia's mind and making her heart race.

"I know this isn't why you summoned me," Anja whispered.

"No..."

"But that's not going to stop you, is it?"

"Only if you want me to stop." Torenia's fingers played with the knotted fabric that held Anja's dress together, but Anja shook her head, kissing Torenia's lips. She nestled her body against Torenia's; they fit together the way only their bodies could. Anja pushed her back onto the table. It rattled, the lantern light sending the shadows into a rampage. She slipped her hand underneath Torenia's skirt, caressing her bare thigh, wringing a husky moan from her throat.

Torenia brought her lips to Anja's neck as she stood between her legs, her soft fingers finding her core. With a gasp, she arched her back and pressed her body firmly against Anja, who held her tight. Her eyes shut, and she lost her sense of surroundings, allowing herself to be at her most vulnerable. When she reached her crescendo, Anja kept her close, nipping at her skin and tangling her fingers in her black hair.

Torenia caught her breath, studying Anja through glassy eyes filled with adoration. Her hand finally tugged the knot securing Anja's dress free, letting it pool around her feet. Torenia stood on shaky legs, letting her dress fall back into place. She took a few steps, pushing Anja against the bookshelves. A long time ago it had been Torenia there, and Ivan in her place. She had taken then; with Anja, she would always give.

"I need everything there is to know about balance," Torenia explained when their clothing was replaced and tousled hair was presentable again. There was no tension in Torenia's shoulders at that moment, and, for that, she was grateful. "Look out for anything mentioning waters running black. I've searched every bit of information we have on the Black Sea; it's given me nothing."

"Very well." Anja eyed the stack of books. "Shall I begin with these?"

"Yes." Torenia nodded, then added, "You cannot let Roman know about this. Not yet. I need...leverage. Knowing Roman, the moment he finds out I'm on Nikolai's scent, he'll take over and claim the discovery as his own."

Anja nodded in agreement and began to skim through the books. In silence, aside from the turning of pages and crackle of the fire, they read page after page, searching for anything that jumped out at them. The hours trickled by as they researched. Torenia wrote down anything that called out to her, though there was little until she found a penned-in legend.

A legend about balance and sirens.

The Seer spoke of balance. Torenia thought it was about the Brotherhood, but now she wondered if it was something else.

"'When the blood is spilled, the balance will return,'" Torenia mumbled, then looked to Anja. "Did you discover anything on sirens?"

"Yes." Anja flipped through the pages of a book she'd set aside and, when she found the page, pushed the book toward Torenia. "Prince Eiríkur of Kæ'vale slaughtered them in droves, eating their flesh until they, presumably, went extinct."

Torenia tapped her fingers on the table, then rose so quickly that the blood rushed to her head. She had seen something like this before. Despite her exhaustion after hours of research, she scoured the depths of her mind. Where had she seen a book of such stories and legends before?

"Oh." She remembered bitterly. "His study."

"Pardon?"

"Anja, I need a diversion..." She drummed her fingers on the desk. "I need you to let someone out of the harvest, but I need you to promise me you will not be caught."

Anja stood, smoothing out her dress. Approaching Torenia, she placed a hand on her waist and trailed her fingers up and down. "I will not let you down. May I ask what you will be doing?"

Torenia hid her nervousness by selecting a book from the table to take with her. "I will be breaking into Roman's study."

Anja looked shocked but didn't argue. She hurried off to the harvest while Torenia raced to Roman's study. If incense was burning, it meant he was there; she had learned over the years. The smell of it, a gentle pine scent, reached her nose. Tucking herself out of sight, she waited for a sign that Anja had completed her end of the task. A young servant came racing down the hall moments later, hammering his fist on the door of Roman's study.

Torenia listened as Roman opened the door, demanding to know the reason behind the disruption, then hastily rushing down the hall. As Torenia slipped in, she noted exactly where everything was, from the chair that had been hastily pushed out from the desk to the book lying open on it. The shelves on the wall beckoned her closer, and she hurried to it. Reading all sorts of titles, her head craned to the side, she felt the pressure of time constraints crushing her.

"There you are," she exclaimed quietly, pulling the little blue book from the shelf. It left a gap that would not go unnoticed, so Torenia replaced it with a book from the library. With one final glance around, she left the study, the book clutched tightly to her body.

"Some believe," Torenia read out loud hours later, when the events of the harvest escapee had died down, *"that when a woman is violently murdered, particularly drowned, she is reincarnated as a Rusalka, otherwise known as a siren.'* His mother was drowned by Roman."

"Nikolai is searching for his mother?" Anja asked. "Kæ'vale is a bit far, is it not? Are we sure it's Kæ'vale?"

"He had to run far if he was to have a chance at escaping his brother." Torenia frowned. "He is seeking redemption, atonement."

"There must be more to it."

Nodding in agreement, Torenia realized what she must do. Having let Nikolai slip from Roman's grasp once, she could not afford another mistake. But, she could not simply inform Roman that Nikolai was wandering about Kæ'vale in search of sirens—for what reason, she did not know—without researching more. Her work was not finished; she had so much more to discover before she went to Roman and proved herself worthy of the title she held weakly in her fingertips. Holding the title of Sister was like trying to grasp sand in her fist; it kept falling through her fingers.

Without another word, she left the library. Her gown swept along the ground as she moved briskly to where she knew she would find Ivan. As expected, he was in the fighting pits where countless human and vampire corpses lay in a heap. Those in the harvest were allowed to try to fight for their freedom. Beside the pile of those who had not survived the fights was the fighting ring. Ivan was there, covered in blood from head to toe, and shirtless. His opponent was on the ground, breathing heavily, trying to get back on his feet.

Torenia did not watch the fights often, as she had her own blood lust satisfied in other, more elegant ways.

Ivan caught sight of her and grinned. Seeing his distraction, his opponent grabbed something from the floor of the pit and attacked Ivan. Torenia watched with vigilance as Ivan reacted. He was too late. The man had a fragment of bone in his grasp and slashed at Ivan with the shard. Despite the blood gushing from the right side of his face, Ivan recoiled with the force of the attack—his feet hardly moved. His reaction was swift, grabbing the bone shard and removing it from his adversary's grip. He plunged the bone deep into the belly of his attacker, ending the fight.

Shouts of approval echoed through the pits as another battle was won. Ivan, dripping with blood from the wound beside his eye, walked over to the edge of the ring. The vampire-filled crowd was still cheering as they filtered out.

"Torenia, it is good to see your face," he said politely. The words sounded wrong coming from someone who was dripping in another man's blood.

"I have a request," Torenia said.

"For you? Anything." Ivan grinned.

Torenia still found herself occasionally longing for Ivan, but that had faded when Anja arrived. She did feel a certain level of trust with him that she did not feel with his brother. Roman was always seeing every angle, distrusting anyone and everyone. Ivan, though, confided in her and broke Roman's rules of staying away from her; she felt a sort of bond with him, which was why she came to him when she needed help.

"I need a siren," she said at last.

"Consider it done."

Torenia nodded in thanks, leaving the pit and Ivan behind her. She had one more thing to do. Without it, there would be no guarantee that her place in the Brotherhood would remain. Her quest for power was coming to an end, it was just within her reach. But with the Brotherhood hanging by such a delicate thread, she considered her other options, what the future of the Brotherhood might look like.

With her in Roman's seat.

33

Torenia could only call it beautiful, but that wasn't quite accurate; the siren before her was dripping with perfection. A creature of the Sea with gills, webbed hands, and a massive tail that darkened in color from her skin, an amber hue. Her upper half was female, with brilliant amber eyes that looked glassy in the lighting of the room. Through the bridge of her round nose were three bones. Her tail and hands were strapped down so Torenia could study her without the threat of being attacked.

"Do you speak?" she asked.

The siren hissed in reply, and she pursed her lips in disappointment. She tried a different tactic. "This would go a lot easier if you spoke. I do not wish to hurt you, but I will not lose sleep over it."

The siren stared back at her with cold amber eyes. That stare told her there would be no reasoning with this creature. She respected the amount of dignity she held, that she would remain silent for the safety of her people. All Torenia knew about these creatures was that a prince in a faraway land enjoyed their flesh, but she dared not take a bite.

She did not believe that Nikolai was searching for sirens to save them, regardless of how righteous he was. She saw no reason behind this—how could it benefit him? If Torenia had learned anything over the years, it was that people made choices that benefitted themselves. Nightwalker, man, siren—selfishness was in every living being's nature. So, she got to work unearthing the mystery; what did Nikolai want with a siren? With knives and blades, phials, and a sharp pair of scissors, Torenia had all she needed. Grabbing the webbed hand of the siren, she spread her fingers and brought a scalpel to the tip of one of them. Blood surged to the surface as the blade broke its skin and instantly Torenia recoiled. It was black and smelled rancid. This confirmed what the Seer had said; where the waters run black.

The siren grinned.

But Torenia was not easily put off by the scent of rank blood. Different people had different-tasting blood; diseased men and women were foul-tasting, and the scent gave them away well before the taste. People who had too much alcohol in their systems also tasted differently. She had heard that pregnant women and children tasted the best.

Torenia rang a bell, and Anja appeared within minutes.

"Bring me one of the kitchen maids. Low-bred, vampire," Torenia commanded. She needed a test subject. "One of Roman's."

"Yes, *Koroleva*."

Anja returned not long later, her hand clutching the collar of a kitchen maid. The maid was shaking; a familiar sight. All the girls in the castle skittered around Torenia in fear of what she might do. Even though she only bathed in the blood of virgins, no one could be sure whether Torenia believed they were virgins or not.

"You've been chosen for something greater," Torenia informed her, crouching in front of the maid where she was seated. Anja stood behind the young woman, hands on her shoulders. Torenia smiled, her bright, red lips suggesting danger. "What is your name?"

The girl kept her lips sealed.

But Anja knew it anyway. "Her name, Torenia, is Aster."

Torenia's eyes jolted up to Anja to see if she was telling the truth. No one, aside from Roman, knew about Aster and the rest of the Luca family; Torenia had kept that part of her life very secret. She grinned at the young woman. "Well, this is going to be *so* much fun."

Torenia stood by the table where the siren lay; the creature had her head to the side, staring at Aster with a glower. Without wasting any more time, Torenia grabbed a large blade and brought it to the forearm of the siren, who bared her teeth in a show of hatred. She did not squirm or try to fight what she knew was inevitable. Torenia respected the show of power and the strength it took to accept a fate like this. Slicing the nearly translucent flesh, she filled a goblet with the viscous fluid.

With a full cup of the night-black blood, Torenia turned to face Aster. The young vampire looked nothing like Torenia's younger sister, but sharing the name helped Torenia overlook any hint of guilt.

She did not hesitate to force Aster to drink from the cup. Before she finished sputtering to try and stop herself from ingesting it, Aster began to react. A shriek emitted from her stained lips, her eyes rolling back into her head as she began to seize. Black froth foamed at her lips, spilling out and dribbling down her chin and neck.

Torenia stepped back, watching as the maid quickly died from what appeared to be blood poisoning. She had never seen anything work that fast, aside from the odd lethal plant like the Hemlock she applied to her lips for the Kiss of Death.

A slow clap came from the cold brick stairs that spiraled to the main level of the castle. Ivan and Roman came in, both vividly impressed with her discovery and how quickly she had reached it. It was Roman clapping. Though Torenia was pleased to be recognized for her ability, she had not wanted this information to reach them until she had achieved an unbreakable bond. She suspected the instructions to do this were contained in the torn-out pages from the Witches Testament and wondered if Roman held them now.

He was a snake in the grass, and she could not trust him to hold her place in the Brotherhood unless she forced his hand.

This had been her bargaining chip.

"Torenia, I *am* impressed," he said boldly, each word accented to prove he was not lying.

"Thank you, Roman," she replied.

Anja nodded to both brothers politely. Though her place was secure with Torenia, Roman and Ivan could do anything they wished.

If they thought she might not be beneficial, that she was not to be trusted, or even looked at them wrong, they could make her disappear. Both Sokolov brothers knew the havoc Torenia would unleash if they laid a hand on her.

"Our baby brother is looking for a siren, so that he may steal her blood and poison us?" Roman asked, walking around the siren, who stared coldly at him.

"I believe so, yes." Torenia wiped her hands on the fabric of her skirt. The floor was covered in blood and dust, among other things she did not wish to identify. She had not yet come to the conclusion that Roman drew so swiftly but, given a few minutes to think, she would have. Roman took that from her, but she needed to take something from him. Her time to reign was nearing.

"And he is in Kæ'vale," Roman declared.

She did not know how Roman had come about this knowledge, but she nodded.

Roman smiled ever so slightly, his fangs visible. "I noticed a book was missing from my study, so I took a look at what you were studying."

Roman never stepped foot in the library, but Torenia should have been better at hiding her studies. He still did not trust her. She pressed her lips tight together, knowing if she allowed herself to speak, she might say something she would regret.

"I want you to continue your research, Torenia. Ivan will find you every last siren if that is what it takes. I want to know everything about them. I want to know their history—if you cannot make them talk, cut out their tongues. Anything you need to prepare us for what we are facing, you have my full support," he said, placing a sharp-nailed hand on her shoulder. "You are so close to earning your place here, Torenia."

34

Torenia dragged out her research for as long as she could; months went by, and she learned everything that there was to know about sirens and how they could harm vampires. Hundreds of sirens lay among the corpses below the pits, and she felt not an ounce of guilt for any of them. Some spoke, but most held their tongues in a show of power, refusing to cave in to their torturer. Even if she offered to free them, they refused to accept her offers; they proved to be an exceptionally stubborn species.

Surrounded by her most trusted maids, with Anja as her advisor, they worked together like gears in clockwork. One of her newest tests had been studying the effects of drinking the blood of man when they had recently consumed Siren. Time after time it had proven to be safe, something that set her mind at ease; she was not usually picky about whom she feasted upon, but one could not stalk their prey for days to ensure they had eaten what was safe for her to have. The harvest was the safest food source, of course, but after a time those bodies began to have a sour aftertaste; she had noticed it a few years back and recently opted for her own source of blood.

Tired from being on her feet all night, Torenia sat down in a grand leather chair. The fine black hide was smooth against her pale skin. Draping her hand over the side, she grabbed a chalice filled with blood and swirled it, trying to think how she could finally elevate her place here. How many years had it been? She had lost count, though she still looked to be in her mid-twenties. Her power was great, but it was not great enough; she refused to be matched. As much as she had once respected Roman, she now wished to tower above him. Though she would never let these words leave her lips—not even to her most trusted maids.

He wanted her to be like Azalea Luca. At the peak of Azalea's power, she was merely the town witch, nothing like Torenia. Yet her name carried over hundreds of years; people heard rumors and whispers of the Luca curse, the legendary Wolf she had created. Her legacy crossed the continent, but it was only in death that her name spread. Torenia refused to be a martyr—she wanted her name to cross borders and people to fear her while she was still alive. Though Azalea Luca was known for creating the Wolf that resided in the forests of Silvania, it was her brutality and willingness to sacrifice her own child for power that made her the legend she was. Roman wanted her to be like Azalea, so Torenia wondered if that was what she must do—be ruthless enough to kill anyone who got in her way. But did Roman understand that he was in her way?

As if in tune with her thoughts, he came down the stairwell. He was humming a tune she'd heard Ivan play on the piano; it had the essence of a lullaby. Stopping at the bottom of the stairs, he continued to hum when Torenia didn't look his way. Her body remained rigid, facing the blood-stained wall.

She set the chalice down harder than she had intended to.

"Lost your appetite?" Roman asked, his taunting voice sounding more like Ivan's than his own. The brothers were similar beyond looks; it came out in their voices and their body language. And yet, Torenia trusted Ivan. Perhaps because Roman told her not to.

She lolled her head to the side to look at him, dumping the blood from the chalice onto the ground, until each drop had fallen into a puddle below before she dropped the cup. Rising from her seat, Torenia grabbed a scalpel and crossed the room in no more than three broad steps. Before Roman could react, she lunged at him and slit his throat. The blood spurted from the wound, covering Torenia until she was drenched. Her relieved laughter filled the room and then—

Torenia was still in her seat, the bloody dream only a fabrication of her fractured mind. Roman was still awaiting an answer from her. Glancing at him, she stood up and sighed. "Roman, there is much more to learn about sirens, I am sure. However, I did not ask for a siren to study them to death, I asked for them to study their effects on vampires. I have done this. I have found Nikolai."

"You're asking what is next?"

She fought hard to avoid scowling. She was not some maid waiting for their next task. Hands clenched at her sides, she allowed only one physical discomfort to show, then released it.

"Yes, Roman, I am," she stated.

"I am leaving for a time. Ivan will be in charge." He was carefully calculating her reaction.

"Ivan?" she inquired. "Not Ivan and I?"

"You heard me the first time, Torenia."

She knew it in her bones; even after waiting for years and being patient, she knew Roman was never going to give her what she wanted. Her decision now could lead to her death, it could lead to banishment or something far worse—and knowing Roman, there was always something worse than death. She had to embrace her Luca roots, but she could not kill Roman. Though the Brotherhood was always balanced precariously, murdering their leader would not do her any good. He would become a martyr and people she could not control would come for her. And though her reputation was beginning to precede her, Roman was the one who put fear into nightwalkers around Osleka.

She had to break him by taking something dear from him. When he snapped, the others would want to see new leadership. That is when she would take the throne.

"Years ago, you promised me power, eternal beauty," she started.

Roman folded his fingers together in front of him. "Do you have power?"

"Some."

223

"Did you discover eternal beauty?" he asked.

"Yes, I learned that myself; you did not give it to me."

He chuckled. "Oh, Torenia, do you think you could have discovered it on your own? Out there with your petty potions and midwifery? You never would have thought of such without that book—"

"A book that should have been in my family," she accused. The first witch to pen her thoughts in the book had been Azalea Luca. "Do not patronize me. You have lied to me about so much."

"And you believed me." He finished the conversation with that. A slap to her face whilst he wore a grin on his. Usually, he was not a smug person, but it appeared as if he loved seeing her grasp at every thread he dangled, and she kept on falling for it. Time and time again, she played his games without question. Just like Nikolai had warned her.

"Yes, *Korol*," she said smoothly, though it felt like acid burning from her lungs and her throat, singeing her tongue on the way out.

After guaranteeing that Roman had left, Torenia had her usual crimson bath and made sure she was in her best condition. Cleaning off the blood, she rubbed honey and rose oil cream into her pale skin. Spending a fair amount of time on her appearance wasn't something she did often; because of her natural beauty, she did not need to adorn herself with makeup and jewelry. But tonight, she was going to. Her hair was left long and straight. Applying crimson lipstick, she finished off her evening appearance with the necklace that Ivan had gifted her.

The best way to win someone over was to appeal to what they wanted most.

Like Roman had done to her. After all, this was his game; the only way she could win was by mirroring his maneuvers.

Her sleek, black gown was more lace than solid; it covered her in places that polite society deemed necessary and was otherwise sheer.

Though it was not one she wore often, it was a gown she adored more than the rest. She knew Ivan loved it, too.

Moving through the halls with grace to her brisk walk, she found Ivan in the pits as expected. Only this time he was fighting Baltazar. The crowd cheered and the sound of the bear roaring echoed in Torenia's ears. Smiling, she knew that she had Ivan wrapped around her finger; they both had the same view of the world and their guilty pleasures.

Baltazar was just his warm-up. While Ivan thrived on chaos and destruction, he had a soft spot for Baltazar. The bear sauntered over, swiping with his massive, clawed paw. Ivan danced out of the way, but the show was not staged. Both Ivan and Baltazar would maul one another, bite through flesh, and tear through muscle. The bear caught Ivan's arm and sent him sprawling. But the vampire, a more feral beast than human, hopped back to his feet in an instant, laughing wildly.

Baltazar roared as Ivan lunged. He swatted as he approached, then opened his jaw wide to bite down on whatever part of Ivan he could. Ivan threw an elbow into the bear's jaw, making the animal shake his head in surprise.

"Come on, do it!" Ivan shouted. "Do it!"

Baltazar managed to get his massive jaws around Ivan's bulky frame, shaking him like a dog would a rabbit, before throwing him aside. Ivan groaned, his shirt shredded, blood oozing out of wounds made by the bear's incisors.

Torenia, watching from the sidelines, rolled her eyes at the theatrics. Baltazar got up on his hind legs and then dropped with all his weight onto his front paws. Ivan rolled out of the way and got back to his feet, then threw half a dozen punches to the animal which only enraged it more. The bear knew better than to let Ivan get behind him, but Ivan was faster. He leaped onto the beast, trapping his neck in a chokehold. Only when Baltazar lay down, giving in, did Ivan hop off and offer his whistle of truce. He tore his ripped shirt off.

Baltazar left the pits with the audience roaring their delight. A ragged-looking man entered, likely one from the harvest fighting for his freedom. Another brawl began, and Torenia watched with slightly less interest. It was a much faster fight; despite Ivan having already taken on a full-grown bear, he was a force to be reckoned with.

He was ruthless.

As the fight came to a swift end, Ivan stood shirtless behind a vampire whose head rolled forward as he could no longer keep it up, Torenia feeling a surge of excitement. Ivan walked around the circle and raised his hands, warranting cheers and shouts from the crowd— lowly vampires. After making his lap around the pit, he faced his opponent and held his jaw in either hand. The blood on the opposing man's face obscured what he might have once looked like before Ivan had beaten him to a pulp. Ivan kissed the man on either cheek and then snapped his neck. But he wasn't done. He knelt over the body, which toppled so that it was impossible for Torenia to see what he was doing.

When Ivan rose again, he held the severed head in his hands, showing it to the crowd; they shouted louder than ever. Tossing the head aside, he was walking towards the exit when he spotted Torenia. Under the arterial spray on his face, a casual smile formed, one that only appeared when he was around her. One might have said it was sweet or smitten if they didn't know him.

"Oh Torenia, how lovely to see your *pretty* face. And might I add that you look *ravishing?*" He flashed her a cheeky grin. "Did you see the fights?"

"Very impressive," she replied honestly.

"What can I do for you tonight?" he asked, though there was so much depth to his question. What would she want this time? Fresh maids to blood? Fine dining on the rich? Or perhaps something more carnal?

"If I ask you something, will you answer honestly?"

"I always do."

"Promise me."

"Torenia, have I *ever* wronged you?"

"No," she stated. "You have not."

"So," he flashed his teeth, "what would you ask of me?"

"What can give me power here? True power?" She knew but

needed someone close to Roman to confirm what she believed would be the final move to place Roman in checkmate.

"That's obvious, Torenia." Ivan grinned. "Take away the thing he loves most."

"Bring me Roman's daughter," she commanded.

35

T he giant doors to the throne room burst open. Ivan walked in
dramatically, tracking in snow and mud from his boots. He
ruthlessly hauled Svetlana behind him, wrapped in a white full-
length fur coat. She looked like a lamb in the jaws of a wolf in his
fierce grip. Her voice was stern as she demanded that he release her,
but Torenia could hear the fear underlying her tone. She could put
on a show for anyone, but Torenia was in tune to that fear; she lived
for it.

"Bring her to me," Torenia commanded, seated shamelessly upon
Roman's throne. Her legs were crossed under a tight-fitting white
gown. The bottom fanned out into a long train, while the top hugged
her figure and turned to lace above her breasts. The lace and boning
of the collar reached her chin, and she wore no sleeves despite the
cold spilling through the open door. Rahella sat behind her, perched
on the back of the throne.

Dropping Svetlana at Torenia's feet, Ivan stepped back and
waited, a hungry look etched into his war-weathered face. The scar
running along the length of his eye from a previous fight had healed
poorly. The disfigurement suited him.

Svetlana braced herself for the impact on the marble floor but
still cried out as she tumbled to the ground. She did not race back to

her feet because she knew that she would be thrown down again. Instead, she leaned back onto her calves and looked up at Torenia. Her hands hung in front of her, anger flashing in her eyes, reminding Torenia of Roman. Knowing she was defeated, the girl did not fight, but the look in her eye said she clearly wished to know why.

"Do you have any idea why I have brought you here tonight?" Torenia asked, her fingernails rhythmically tapping along the end of the throne's arm. Her hands were adorned with rings.

"To kill me?" Svetlana spat.

"Well yes, although that is not the *reason,* dear girl."

"Do not speak like my father. You may sit on his throne, but if he were here he would not hesitate to kill you."

"When you first arrived, I knew you would take my place if I did not get rid of you," Torenia explained. "I made you so power-hungry that you knew nothing else, but you were not smart enough to control that hunger. We are not so different, you and I—we have the same *desire* for power. But you attacked Roman headfirst with your greed. It got rid of you, yes, for the time being. It opened up an opportunity for me to climb higher, but not high enough. There was always the possibility that Roman would hand the title to you, all that power simply because you were born *pure.*" She spat the final word.

"Now, here we are." Torenia gestured around her. "I still need to be rid of you. I need to break Roman in order to achieve the power I desire. I must remove what gets in my way."

"You would let her do this to your brother, Ivan? To your niece?" Svetlana turned to look at her uncle, who stood passively to the side, observing.

"Roman's power has grown too great. He takes, but he does not give," Ivan explained, surprising Torenia most of all. "I am an equal, and yet I am not."

"You could not be equal to him, either of you!" Svetlana screamed. "You think you will be alive after he finds out about this?"

Torenia rolled her eyes. Ivan was on her side, far more than she had anticipated, and for that she was grateful. Roman might very well have killed her if she had attempted this on her own, but to have Ivan beside her was ideal. Roman couldn't manage the Brotherhood without both of them at his side; it was precariously balanced and had been for years. There had been a period of calm but, as of late, the turmoil had been too great for Ivan and Roman to pursue Nikolai, who still roamed the continent in search of sirens. Many vampires chose solitary lives with no desire to be governed. Roman would fail should he slaughter the only two people who stood beside him.

It was her time to strike.

Torenia rose from her seat and descended the steps to stand before Svetlana. She tucked a hand underneath her chin, lifting her face so that she could look her in the eyes. Torenia studied her. Jealousy coursed through her veins; ancient, something she had not felt for many years. Yet here it was again, exhumed, burning bright inside her. Svetlana's bright blue eyes were a trademark of the Sokolovs, her porcelain skin and round face to the liking of every man and woman. There was no denying her graceful beauty.

"I am going to kill you now, Svetlana. But first, you must answer me one question."

Lana jerked from Torenia's grasp, but Ivan caught her quickly, holding her in place. His grip pinched her shoulder so tight that she cried out. Tears slid down her face.

Torenia did not hesitate to backhand the girl, her rings leaving gashes on her cheek. Blood dribbled down her right cheek, blending with the tears and turning a watery crimson. Svetlana sobbed, fighting Ivan's grip to no avail.

"A pity. I wanted to leave you pretty, for Roman's sake," Torenia said, her voice filled with disappointment. "At least he will know that you put up a fight."

"He's going to tear you limb from limb." Svetlana shook her head as she spoke, her voice shaking but bravery still evident in her posture.

"Perhaps," Torenia said as she knelt. "Tell me, Lana—have you laid with anyone?"

"No."

"Perfect." Her lips were ever close to Svetlana's.

Lana's eyes grew wide. "I have the antidote, your poison cannot kill me."

"Hemlock is not what is on my lips," Torenia replied, a smile on her black lips. "Siren's blood is much more potent."

Leaning closer, Torenia kissed her.

When Svetlana gasped, her tongue touched the poison. She took a shuddering breath as the poison entered her system. She gagged as her throat closed, beginning to choke as no air entered her lungs. With her hands at her sides, she clutched her fingers into her palms to avoid looking desperate. She truly was Roman's daughter, frantic to appear brave and strong until the end. She finally collapsed forward and writhed until her body went limp.

Torenia used her foot to push Svetlana's body over so she was on her back and straddled the cadaver. Even in death, with black froth spilling from her mouth, she was still beautiful. The blood on her cheek was still wet with tears. Wide eyes stared at Torenia as she glared back.

Torenia wiped the siren blood and layer of wax she'd applied to prevent it from touching her lips, then reached her hand back and commanded Ivan. "Knife."

When the smooth hilt of a freshly sharpened blade was in her grasp, she slid it along Svetlana's clavicle, then down between her breasts. Peeling back the skin, Torenia used the knife to pry open the sternum, cracking any ribs that got in her way. It took all her strength, but she refused to give the task to Ivan. She severed the arteries and pulled out the girl's heart. She could feel its phantom beat in her hand, imagining it was still pumping blood through Svetlana's veins.

Torenia placed the heart to the side gently, then began to lather herself in the blood. It was still warm, the best way to apply to obtain the maximum effect. When she was covered, she grabbed the heart and stood. Without looking back at Ivan, she walked straight to Roman's throne.

She sat back down, crossed her legs, and waited for Roman to walk through the door with his daughter's heart growing cold in her palm.

36

Svetlana's death had not lost its novelty by the time Roman walked through the throne room doors. They swung wide against his forceful shove, letting in the cold winter air. Everything was where Torenia had left it. A trail of melted snow and dirt tarnished the usually clean throne room entrance. As did the pile that was Svetlana's body, blood and what resembled a fur coat underneath.

There was no overlooking Torenia, either; she made sure she was the first thing he saw after he assessed the gruesome state of the throne room.

Every inch of her was covered in blood except her piercing blue eyes. In her hand was the heart, dripping blood onto the steps of the throne. The smell of it overpowered all else. Roman's eyes landed on Torenia and he held them there, assessing what she had done, before they gravitated towards his brother. Ivan sat on the lower throne, his own, perched with one foot on the seat, the other on the arm. His hands were draped over his knee as he leaned forward with obvious excitement for what was about to come.

When Roman reached the cadaver on the floor, studying the face of his daughter, colorless and smeared with sprays of blood, Rahella quirked

Undisturbed, Roman looked up and spoke. "Finally."

"Pardon me?" Torenia was unable to mask the shock from her cold voice.

"I have been waiting years for you to prove your ruthlessness," he told her casually, as if it was right before her eyes, obvious since the moment she had accepted his offer all those years ago. His hands spread wide, and his arms reached out to gesture at the body, the bloodshed, the building all around them, all while his eyes were upon Ivan. "It took some coaxing from my dear brother, but not much."

"You mean to tell me you *wanted* me to do this?"

"Everything you have ever done has been because I wanted you to do it."

"That is a lie," Torenia growled, her hand squeezing the heart a little tighter. Blood gushed from her grip. "You cannot stand there and tell me that you wished for me to discover eternal beauty. The look upon your face when you saw that I had bathed in your spy's blood..."

"You discovered that in a book, did you not?"

"Yes."

"A book strategically placed so that you would find it. Find it and learn from all the witches who came before you. You had your doubts about bathing in virgin blood, and Ivan pointed you in the right direction. Just as I told him to do," Roman explained.

"You were enraged when I killed Irina," Torenia recalled. "You might not have shown it the way most men would, but you are no ordinary man."

"No, Torenia, I am not," Roman agreed. "I learned that you were discovering a darker side to yourself, but it was not enough. So I made you believe I was angry, upset about some poor girl. She was nothing but food, *Koroleva*. I put Svetlana in your hands, I offered her up to you like steak to a dog. You pitted her against me, yes, but I wanted you to take your rightful place beside Ivan and I, and I needed to know you were as ruthless as your ancestors, who proved they would stop at nothing for power. I needed to ensure that you were a true Luca, and you have proven yourself time and time again as worthy of the title. I wanted you to rip her heart out. Torenia, I am proud. The Pure Bloods might be vicious, but us Half Bloods will do anything to keep our place."

He paused, before continuing on. "Do you know what Azalea Luca did to her own daughter?"

"Of course I know," Torenia snapped.

"You had no daughter, so I had to use my own to test your limits. I made you think I cared for her. *'Someone very dear to me.'*"

Torenia shook. Her knees wobbled, but they did not buckle. Turning her head to look at Ivan, grinning as he always was, she found herself shocked that he had betrayed her like this.

"Ah, yes." Roman brought the attention back to him. "Ivan was playing you. He has only once betrayed me, but has otherwise only done as he was told."

Torenia looked to Ivan. "I thought—"

"That I was smitten with you?" Ivan asked, finally speaking. He snickered. "I was, and might I add, still am. However, other than the one, or two," his glance slipped to Roman guiltily, "times where I simply *could not* contain myself, it was all for show. You had to believe you had me wrapped around your finger or you would never have asked me to bring back Roman's daughter. You needed to know you would have support if you betrayed Roman."

"Why did you care that we slept together?"

"Conflict of interest. I told you not to trust him, Torenia," Roman reminded her.

She glared at Roman. "Was she even your daughter?"

"Yes." Roman walked towards Torenia. "But she could never have been a queen."

She did not know what he was going to do, but she stood stock still until he was two stairs below her. Pausing, as though time had frozen for a few moments, he studied her. Then, Roman reached out his gloved hand.

"Come, *Sister.*"

37

THE YEAR OF THE BLACK TIDE

Ten Years Later

S he bore the markings of the Brotherhood, dark tattoos along her back and neck. More importantly, she had the equality and the power she was once promised. No longer did she feel the need to usurp Roman, but instead to take over what he had when his inevitable death came knocking. With the lower vampires looking up to her as a leader now, it would be easy to make the changes when Roman was gone.

For years, she had sat as a true equal upon the throne. Leading, giving commands, stopping all-out wars, and managing the harvest. Everything that came with the power she had handled as well as Ivan or Roman ever could. It was clear that neither of them regretted giving Torenia the power she had asked for, the power she deserved. She had earned her place.

Though Torenia would never fully trust Roman or Ivan—or anyone for that matter – she learned to live with what had happened. The Sokolovs had only wanted those with power to be strong, and she respected them for that.

In Roman's study, they discussed the future of the Brotherhood.

"It has been nearly ten years since Nikolai escaped," Roman said, though for the first time, he did not look to Torenia to remind her that she was to blame. It did not matter anymore. Instead, he commended her. "We have replaced him with someone who can stomach what we do for the greater good. It is time that we bring Nikolai home; it is time that he be laid to rest."

"We're going to kill our baby brother?" Ivan asked excitedly.

"And this time we will succeed," Roman said.

"When do we leave?" Torenia asked. She had informed them that Nikolai was still in Kæ'vale; the confirmation came from the Seer. According to her, Nikolai did not stray from the southern edges of the country except when he went north, delivering sirens to safety. Rahella had found the location and reported back to Torenia—she had the power to inform Roman exactly where he would, eventually, find his brother.

"No, my dear, you will not be coming. As valuable as you would be with us, you are needed here," Roman told her. He pressed his gloved hand against her smooth, unaged cheek. "You will be running the Brotherhood until our return."

She nodded, holding back her surprise.

"And Torenia? Should we not return, we leave it in your capable hands," Roman informed her. "We are finally able to pursue Nikolai, knowing the Brotherhood is stable with you in our place."

Torenia tried not to look surprised but failed. "Promise it."

"I promise."

"I mean an unbreakable bond." She had never found the pages missing from the book but had discovered the spell on her own. She had already created one similar when she bound herself to Anja and the others.

He eyed her cautiously; she suddenly realized that Ivan and Roman never had the missing pages from the Witches Testament. It was a bond used by witches around the world to secure their safety from those who wished to burn them alive. It kept them safe, and the prosecutor's family alive and uncursed. She wondered who possessed the missing pages.

"It's a blood bond that ties us to our promise," she said. She held out her palm and withdrew a blade.

Roman pulled off his glove and held out his hand. Torenia slid the blade over the smooth skin of her palm, watching the flesh split like an overripe grape. Blood gushed and she handed the dagger to Roman, who followed her actions.

"The Brotherhood will fall in my command should you not return," Torenia said. Roman bowed his head in agreement. "*Alligant dictum sanguine nostro.*"

"*Alligant dictum sanguine nostro,*" Roman repeated.

Then they repeated the words together.

The magic pulsed through them, binding them to eternally uphold the vow they had made.

"Brother." Torenia nodded respectfully.

"Sister," he replied, before leaning in and whispering to her. "Shall we fail to return, beware the Old Bloods, *Koroleva.*"

Anja was still naked on the bed when Torenia finished her bath. Draped in a robe, she tightened the belt around her waist and looked at the scars all over Anja's body from her life before Torenia took her in. Some were clearly accidental, some made by others.

Now no one touched Anja.

Except Torenia.

"They have been gone for a month, Torenia." Anja rolled onto her side and watched as Torenia selected something to wear.

"The travel time was to take more than that," Torenia reminded her. "I will not send Rahella on another excruciatingly long journey just to see if Roman and Ivan are still alive. She will go when they need her eyes."

"You are not concerned?"

"If they return, everything will go back to normal. If they do not return, I can handle what they have left to me," Torenia said, as she brought one gown to her body, then another before deciding upon something practical, a long-sleeved gown to keep her warm. "And should they not return, I would like you to be by my side."

Anja's eyes widened as she searched for words worthy enough to speak. Torenia raised her hand to stop her from scrambling. "You have more than earned my trust, and I will need someone like you next to me."

"I would be honored," Anja replied at last.

Thinking about Anja's scars, she wondered what else there was in her past that was dark. Though Torenia felt very little, she did care for her. Over the years she had earned her trust, enough that she shared a bed with her, enough that she shared her desires and secrets with her. She pondered who would take that third throne and recalled Tasia speaking up in support of something more than a Brotherhood.

A Sisterhood.

After all, should Roman and Ivan not return from their little excursion to hunt down Nikolai, Torenia would have the Brotherhood. A larger monopoly was manageable with the right people by her side. She thought of Anja, who had strength from her hardship—Torenia understood and respected that. She was also wise and spoke candidly. Torenia suspected Tasia would stand alongside her.

"Does your past haunt you, Anja?" Torenia asked, sliding the gown around her frame. She stepped over to her vanity and opened the drawer, fingering the handle of the mirror from her childhood. The handheld mirror was ornate where she was from, but in this castle, it looked quaint. She looked at her reflection, seeing the version of herself she once saw in the mirror when she was just a girl. She wondered if her younger self would be proud of who she had become.

"I think nothing of my past, only my future, Torenia." Anja gracefully got off the bed, draping the sheet around her muscular body like a makeshift dress. She stood behind Torenia and rested her chin upon her shoulder, her strong arms wrapped around Torenia's middle.

"I often think about my home, what remains. What has become of it since I left." She picked up the handheld mirror, keeping her eyes on her reflection.

"There is no good in dwelling on the past." Anja kissed her cheek.

"No." Torenia put the mirror back down too firmly and watched the glass fracture. "I suppose not."

She shut the drawer.

In the library, only a mere hour before the sun was to rise, Torenia ran her fingers along the ancient ink. The huge book, to which she had added so many of her own discoveries, felt displaced. Though it belonged in the hands of a Luca, yes, it felt wrong not being with the bones of her ancestors where the Wolf now lingered. Part of her understood the distance; it was best to keep all these things separate so that someone with ill intent did not end up with all that power. To have the book and the Wolf would be to have control over not just Silvania, but so much more.

Perhaps extending her grasp a little further might not hurt.

"*Rahella,*" she whispered to the winds.

When the great bird gripped the windowsill with fierce talons, she rose her head tall and looked right at Torenia, awaiting orders. Torenia stepped up to the raven, running her hand along the muscular body, feeling the sleekness of her wings; the connection between them sent a ripple through the air.

"Bring home here to me," she told Rahella.

Then she waited.

Seventeen years had gone by since Torenia had seen Silvania. Something had changed; she could still feel the hatred in the air, seeping into her flesh and deep in her veins, but it was fading. The taste of it lingered on her tongue from years passed, like spoiled blood. Snow fell softly, covering the town in a blanket. It was exactly how she had left it; cold. A few new homes popped up along the muddy paths, their warm lights glowing in the night.

Rahella diverted from the main road to the cemetery, which was dark with crumbling headstones. The names and dates of the deceased were carved crudely, some of them no longer legible. Not a single stone had flowers or anything to suggest anyone had come to mourn. The dead were gone, they ceased to matter. When their bodies were laid into the ground, the maggots and fungus took them back, bugs feasting on their decaying flesh until they were nothing more than dust and bones.

The dates on Torenia's parent's graves matched; both had died in the same year, the date not specified. Fifteen years ago. They had died young. She hoped it had been slow and painful, filling them with regret about how they had lived their lives.

Leaving the cemetery, Rahella flew to the familiar Luca home; it stood tall and untarnished, well taken care of. They had power and money. The land was larger and had merged with the neighboring property. Rahella perched, waiting for hours, until the sun rose to brighten the world.

It was the only time Torenia was able to see the sun now.

From the back door came a herd of children, three strapping young boys and a girl whose age fit somewhere in the middle. The eldest boy—about fifteen—went straight to chopping the firewood for the morning, the second youngest to the well for water. The youngest of the four children, perhaps twins, went to the garden and salvaged for winter peas, some garlic. They giggled and laughed, the first sign of anything resembling joy in the family and the town itself.

The sight was unsettling.

Aster stepped out of the home with a babe on her breast. She surveyed her children with a sternness that made her look exactly like their mother. The children stopped laughing, and continued their chores, but there was no unhappiness and hatred there.

Finally came the father of this congregation of children.

His soft hair had grayed, salt and pepper at his temples. He still bore a youthful appearance and a strong physique. His arm wrapped around Aster, who leaned into her husband and accepted that warmth with a smile on her pretty face.

Adam looked so pleased with what he had accomplished—his family, his home.

But there was terror when he saw the raven perched on the scarecrow, the bird fearless.

Torenia grinned. "It's time to go home."

38

S he was home at last.
    Torenia pulled her black hood over her head to hide her face from any onlookers. She did not look the same as when she had left this wretched town, but she did not look as old as she should have. In fact, she looked ten years younger than she was. She felt it, too; not a single ache in her bones. A wicked grin crept onto her pale face when she thought of how Aster would react, with early graying hair, arms, and breasts beginning to sag, her age prematurely catching up to her due to the stresses of provincial life.

The moon shone bright that early evening, an autumn chill in the air that was so bitter it would have made anyone shudder. The town had always been cold. The brightness of the moonlight was close to sunlight; though the sun had set a half hour prior, it still cast a faint brightness.

Torenia knew the way as though she had never left; not a single thing had changed aside from a few new homes. She always wondered why anyone would move to this dreadful town and concluded that they must be hiding from something or someone. They brought anger and hatred with them; it seeped into them like a curse over the town. A curse placed on it by Azalea Luca, amplified by each spiteful family.

Seeing the house, larger now than it had been when she lived there, made Torenia pull back on the reins of the horse. It reared its head back, coming to a stop. As Torenia dismounted, she stroked the neck of the beast beside her, and whispered an incantation; the horse bowed its head, calming down, and she knew it would be right where she left it when she returned.

The previously small family home had doubled in size to fit the children that Aster and Adam had. She wondered how long it had taken for Aster to get pregnant, how long before Adam had to marry her, how long before they inherited the home and began adding to it when she got pregnant again. The thought made Torenia grimace; she had never expected such a mundane life for Aster. But she supposed her sister had never sought to learn that there was more out there. Even dabbling in witchcraft had only been to scare Torenia. She wanted to be perfect and, by their parent's standards, she was.

A shrill scream from the backyard made Torenia recoil, disturbed by the shrieking laughter of children. It was a noise she had never enjoyed. Though it was often said that a woman could feel her maternal instinct whenever a child cried, it only made Torenia raise her lip in disgust, something inside her shriveling. She could not remember the last time she had been near a child.

Carefully, so she would not be seen, Torenia made her way to the backyard. She kept to the forest lining the property, darting behind the trees, appearing and disappearing. The screams of laughter and children playing continued; they did not sense the danger. All four of them were there, unattended, unaware.

She hovered at the edge of the forest, staring at them all, wondering what she would do to them. A rumble in her abdomen told her she was hungry, deprived of a fresh food source the past days. Wrapping her hand around her stomach, as though she were with child, she grinned delightfully at the thought. Children didn't trigger her maternal instincts, but hunger, for their blood was purest. Their joy was foreign to her. How they could laugh, smile, and play when their mother was Aster astounded Torenia.

Perhaps in all that hatred, they found some joy and clung to it.

Perhaps Aster was happy.

"Now, we cannot have that," she muttered to herself.

"Have what?" a young voice asked.

Torenia looked down at the child who had approached her. The male twin; his hair was the curly mess like Adam's had been, with Aster's brown eyes. Scowling at the child for a moment, she swept that approach aside and replaced it with a sickeningly sweet grin.

"Hello child," she said. "What is your name?"

"Constantin, ma'am."

"Well, aren't you polite?" Torenia crouched down and made herself eye level with him. She guessed him to be about eight.

"Mama tells us to always be polite, even to strangers." He spoke flawlessly, enunciating each word.

"Your mother must be a very smart woman," Torenia suggested, hiding the surprise that Aster, of all people, gave such rules to her children when she had been a stuck-up brat all her life.

The boy just nodded, then asked, "What is your name, ma'am?"

"Torenia." She tested the waters, trying to see if he would react. What had Aster told them of their wicked aunt?

The boy's eyes widened in fear, and Torenia was filled with joy. It filled her heart to know that Aster feared Torenia so much that she had told her offspring about her, years after she had disappeared. She grabbed Constantin's wrist as he turned to run away and pulled him back. Her sharp teeth sunk into the soft, untouched flesh of his neck. He could not scream as she devoured him, sucking every last drop of his blood; his tiny body held so little compared to what she was used to, and she knew that she could devour the rest of them as well without feeling full.

She continued to hold the small corpse when she was done, blood lust coursing through her veins. Lifting the boy, she carried him down the hill to the yard where the other children were still playing, unaware of her and unaware that their brother had run off in the first place. Children could be perceptive and so naïve too.

It was the girl who noticed Torenia, and she rushed over shouting. "Constantin!"

When she was close enough, Torenia laid the body down, and the other siblings came to see. They did not know what she had done and simply thought she was returning their brother, although they couldn't tell what state he was in. All three rushed forward like a tiny cavalry. The eldest crouched down and felt for a pulse, then looked up at Torenia.

"What happened!?" His eyes were lit with suspicion. He was older and less naïve than his siblings.

"Oh, children, is that any way to speak to your aunt after all this time?" She pouted.

The eldest rose, speaking urgently to the others. "Mikel, Camellia, go inside and get Mother and Father."

Torenia licked her lips. The back of her ringed hand came into contact with the eldest boy, who was not expecting the blow. As he fell, clutching his cheek, Torenia rushed after the children who had remained stone-still, despite their brother's command, until she had struck him. She caught them with ease, her steps taking her so much farther than their little legs. She grabbed the boy, no older than five, and pinned him down, sinking her teeth into his little throat. His legs kicked furiously for a few seconds before stopping altogether.

Torenia dove for Camellia, but the eldest tackled her and they rolled through the grass and snow before Torenia easily overpowered him and pinned him to the ground. She straddled his torso to keep him down and drained him of his blood before the girl could get up, throwing her head back as blood spurted everywhere. In a semicircle, it flew up over her and splatted the snow, the remainder dribbling down her chin.

The girl shrieked and sobbed, sinking into the snow on her knees.

Torenia rose, shoving the body of the older boy aside, and moved towards the girl.

"My babies!" Aster's shrill voice echoed through the woods. "My babies! What have you done!"

Torenia turned. "Hello, sister."

39

A ster screamed in fear, covering her mouth and stepping back into the doorway, where she came into contact with Adam. He held her shoulders for a moment, looking at Torenia with terror as he saw his children. He pushed past Aster and collapsed beside the oldest boy, shouting something incoherent.

Torenia grabbed the terrified little girl, Camellia, and pulled her to her feet. Standing behind the girl, she crouched and brought her hand around the girl's lithe neck. Aster pushed herself out from the doorway in pursuit of her sister and Adam rose as well, shaking, ready to attack.

"One move and I'll slit her throat," Torenia warned. "You know, Mama always told us not to play after dark."

Aster stopped, standing right next to her deceased little boy, Mikel.

A wail came from the house; the fifth child. Torenia would leave that one alone; she had decided that before she came to Silvania. She knew exactly what she would bestow upon that tiny child, the little girl that would grow up without siblings, her family torn apart. After seeing how joyous the other children were, she knew that the youngest would not fare quite so well. She would be tormented; she would blame her father, the hatred would rip the family apart. It was the Luca tradition; it was in their blood. Not one of them could escape that.

"What did you name her? Your youngest?" Torenia asked.

"You will pay for this." Aster's lip trembled as she spoke.

Torenia clutched the girl's throat and she choked, sobbing. She could smell the fresh urine as it traveled down her leg, melting the snow at their feet. Though Torenia was disgusted by the display of fear, she felt the power that came from it.

Adam raised his hands in defense. "Heather! We named our youngest Heather."

"Keeping the tradition; mother and father would be so proud. I'm curious, did you kill them?"

"Yes," Aster admitted, seeing that obeying what Torenia said would possibly keep the rest of their family alive. She looked at her daughter. "Camellia, it's going to be okay, honey; it's going to be okay."

Torenia asked, "Was it slow?"

"Poison. They died in their sleep," Aster told her, directing her attention back to her sister.

Torenia rolled her eyes back into her head, then groaned. "Forgive me if I fall asleep. What a bore."

"They were going to banish me," Aster admitted.

"For getting pregnant by the farm boy next door?"

"Yes." Aster nodded, tears sliding down her cheeks. They were red from the nipping cold, but she did not appear to feel it. After all these years, the two sisters had changed so much. Aster had gone from being absolutely wretched to a loving mother and wife. All Torenia wanted as a child had been acceptance from her family, but Aster had forced her away and turned their family against her.

She had found no family in the Brotherhood, not one she could trust, but had attained so much more. Looking at Aster, at the weak state she was in because she had allowed herself to finally feel love for something, Torenia felt no sympathy for what she was about to do. She crouched down behind the trembling girl, brushing Camellia's loose hair back so that it was behind her small neck, Torenia poised to bite.

"Don't!" Adam yelled. "Please, Torenia, don't touch my baby girl."

"I recall the day you were scared I would become pregnant. And yet your oldest is—was—what, fifteen years old?" Torenia snarled. "What did Aster say to make you want her child?"

"Aster cared about me, Torenia. You never did."

Torenia blinked. "She may have developed feelings for you, but Aster only ever slept with you to get back at me. She always wanted what I had, and more."

"That's where you're wrong, Torenia," Adam said, his voice teetering. "I loved Aster before I even met you, her beauty was impossible to ignore. But you approached first. I did not think I had a chance with her."

It stung, more than she wanted to admit. She bit her tongue to hold back a rash outburst, pausing only for a moment to collect the pain and hide it deep down where it could not touch her.

"Adam, did your mother never tell you that a little white lie could save a life?" Torenia asked. She did not wait for his answer, sinking her teeth into the girl's neck.

Aster and Adam screamed and rushed towards Torenia. She drank enough just to kill the girl, not draining her entirely. Throwing the body aside, she prepared for a physical fight, having spilled blood everywhere. It covered Aster, who got there first, collapsing next to her daughter and clutching her, desperate to feel life in her body one more time.

Adam came for Torenia, but she easily ducked the blow he threw at her. She pivoted on her foot and slipped out of his range, then lunged forward and grabbed his arm. She shoved it behind his back and felt the joints reaching their limits. He screamed in pain but was not ready to give up, twisting out of her grip and lunging, attacking her at the hips.

They fell to the snow and Torenia grinned. "Just like old times."

"You're a monster!" He brought his fist back to gain power.

"Oh, I know."

He stared down at Torenia, unable to make his fist connect with her jaw.

"Adam!" Aster cried. "Do it!"

She gave him the power he needed. His fist came down, but

Rahella intercepted the blow, clawing at Adam's face with her razor-sharp talons. He raised his hands to protect his face, but the bird was too close and too strong. Recoiling, he fell back into the mixture of blood and snow, punching and kicking at the bird.

"Rahella, enough." Torenia got back to her feet, brushing snow from her coat.

"What do you want from us!?" Aster yelled, suddenly at Adam's side, helping him to his feet.

His face was bloody, his right eye swollen and gushing. She doubted he would ever see out of it again. He leaned on Aster for support, both of them knowing there was nothing they could do. Torenia and Rahella were untouchable. Torenia knew it too, standing tall and smiling brightly. There was blood all over her hands, arms, and face.

Inside, baby Heather cried out.

"Oh yes, there is one more."

"Don't you touch her!" Aster screamed, chasing after Torenia.

By the time Aster reached the house, Torenia held Heather in her arms. She cooed at the baby, despite her hatred for them, rocking her back and forth. The infant stared wide-eyed at the stranger, her big brown eyes just like her mother's. She had perfect porcelain skin and pink lips that were just right. Soft brown locks were growing in, the smoothest hair Torenia had ever felt.

Adam hobbled in and closed the door behind him so that he did not have to look at his dead children.

"Take my life, not hers," Aster begged. "Please, Torenia, if you have any good in your heart. You've already taken everything from me."

"Me?" She laughed bitterly. "Where was the good in your heart when you took everything from me? My home? My parents? My *lover*? The brothel? The only safe place I had. You took the good from my heart, Aster." She paced around the room, the baby in her arms.

"Every day you stripped more and more of it from me until I was nothing! Nothing but hatred and anger, just like this town always wanted. The hatred always wins. You thought it stopped when you found love, when you bore children and discovered that being a mother was a whole new kind of love. But if you had had any decency and *goodness* in your heart, you would have killed me. To spare me from the relentless hatred mother showed me. Where was *your goodness,* Aster?"

"I am sorry, sister." Aster's voice shook.

Torenia was taken aback by the apology. She looked down at Heather. She hadn't planned on killing the youngest, but they did not know that. "Your life for hers."

"No!" Adam protested.

"That's enough, Adam. There is no bargaining with a witch and whatever else she is."

Torenia placed Heather back into the handcrafted wooden crib. Face to face, Aster looked at her sister.

"How did you remain so beautiful?" Aster asked.

"Remain?"

"You were always the prettier one."

"Kneel." Torenia's voice wavered.

Aster knelt, looking up at her sister. Torenia leaned down and kissed either side of her cheeks, then her forehead. Aster had caused her so much pain; she did not deserve to have a happy ending. None of them did. Torenia knew her time would come, though it would be many, many years. She hoped, one day, she would die on her own terms.

Aster let her tears fall as Torenia withdrew her weapon—the shard of glass from the mirror she had taken from this home so many years ago. She brought it to Aster's neck, standing behind her.

"*Please,* Torenia, don't do this," Adam begged. "I beg of you, don't do this!"

It was another taste of power, watching someone grovel; she could never grow tired of it.

"Goodbye, sister."

Torenia slit Aster's throat, watching her blood spill on the hardwood floors.

40

"Why?" Adam finally spoke, not even lifting his bloodied head. He kept it facing downwards, blood dripping from the wounds to his eye and cheek. His arms dangled in front of him— weak, defeated.

Torenia wiped the blade on her sleeve and sheathed it. She turned and glanced out the window; there were trinkets and gifts lining the sill. To her right, by the familiar hearth, was a bookshelf. Crossing the living room, she found the old book of myths and legends that Mama used to read to them when they were children. She opened it to the page of the Luca legend, the Wolf that was tethered to them for eternity. There were books around the continent depicting their family line. It was no wonder that Roman sought her out.

"Why?" Adam asked louder this time. "After all this time, why return now?"

"I was curious." She dragged out the last word, her voice bouncing like Roman's did. Torenia held the book in her hands, turning to face Adam now.

"Curious?" Adam looked up at last. "You're a witch."

"Yes, I am," Torenia agreed. Then she slammed the book shut, waltzing over to the cradle once more. She looked at Heather and grinned wickedly. "Did you know that hatred runs in our blood?"

"Yes," he replied, for he had heard her say it before.

Reaching into the crib, she stroked Heather's smooth cheek. "Three hundred years ago my ancestor killed one child and cast away the other. It created a rift in the delicate balance of family, you see. Family is supposed to be full of love, unconditionally. But her evil, her need for power, created a spiteful family, a poison she never meant for her own family to drink. I could feel, when I looked upon your *precious* family, that the poison had run out. But tonight, I recreated it. It will continue; you will raise this child, and she will come to loathe you and you her.

"You will never trust your own daughter, and one day she may kill you, just as Aster killed our parents. She will be hated by all in this town, as all Lucas are. You cannot stop what I have started here, no matter how you raise her or how far you run. It's in your blood now."

"Just leave." Adam stared at her. "Just leave us."

"Very well," she agreed. Clasping her hands together, she walked over to him. He recoiled as she knelt down in front of him and kissed his forehead. "Goodbye, Adam."

"I have called you both here to discuss something quite delicate," Torenia said to Anja and Tasia. She leaned against Roman's desk in his study, the sturdy wood supporting her. A fire crackled in the hearth next to them.

Anja sat on the arm of one of the chairs, while Tasia stood nearer to the door—searching for a quick exit.

Torenia flipped her palm and held it out to the two vampires. She gauged Tasia's reaction first, for she suspected that Anja already knew. When Torenia had woken at midday a few months prior, with an ache in her hand that burned like hot coals, she had known what it meant. She now held the power of the Brotherhood in her palms, and she was going to make changes.

"I believe the Sokolov line has ended," she told them.

"What does that mean for the Brotherhood? They govern nearly all the vampires in the country," Tasia said.

Torenia smiled wryly. "I suspect many will be disappointed to find that Roman has left the Brotherhood to me."

"Nothing a weak man fears more than a woman with power," Anja said.

"We must make Roman's death come across as a sacrifice. He must become the god that his flock believed him to be. They will not take kindly to me taking his power—I don't think the masses will ever be entirely pleased with who sits upon the throne. Pure Blood, Half Blood, man, woman. No matter who sits there, they will try to tear them down."

"Their deaths were noble, then." Tasia crossed her arms.

"We will present them that way." Torenia nodded. "Now, onto more important matters. We can sort out the nitty-gritty of how to properly announce the passing of Roman and Ivan later. What I wish to speak to you two about now is far more important, a ripple of change. Tasia, remember the seed we planted?"

"Of course," Tasia replied with a smile. "You certainly know how to bide your time. Not all of us can stay young forever."

Torenia laughed lightly. "I apologize for the delay. I do hope it is worth it. I need you two by my side, to rule with me. Ruling is not a task for one; it is a collaborative effort. I cannot do it without you both. And, before you agree or disagree, talk amongst yourselves without me here—"

Anja stood up. "I pledged my loyalty to you with my blood. I give my love to you with my body and my heart. I need not discuss the matter, I know where I stand."

Torenia's heart thundered a little harder. So many years of fighting for this, so many days without feeling love and affection—it swelled now inside her, threatening to pour out of her like blood from a wound.

"It should come as no surprise that I will stand beside you as an equal," Tasia said. "A Brotherhood falls, but a Sisterhood rises from the ashes."

~

Before her was a sea of black. Thousands of vampires from around the country, and even beyond their borders, knelt before her. Each of them had their black hoods pulled over their heads in mourning, heads bowed in unanimous sadness. The row of guards separated the crowd of nightwalkers from the three who sat upon the thrones.

Torenia scanned the crowd, looking at all of those affected by the deaths of Roman and Ivan. After she had found Roman's body, she located Ivan's in a house a few hours away from the cove. She collected what she needed from both of them, odds and ends for talismans and spells.

Beside her sat Anja and Tasia, their shoulders back and heads high. They had power they never expected or wanted, but when Torenia offered them the chance to change the world, they both accepted without hesitation.

Rising from her seat, she looked down as thousands of eyes met hers.

"Roman would have been proud!" she exclaimed, gesturing to all those below her. "To see so many faces in mourning, all of you who have come together in this time of sorrow, this time of humility, to face our mortality. But his death has not left us without control, without order. No, his death has opened a flood of opportunity. Opportunity to work together, to mend our wounds, and move forward in light of this tragedy.

"Roman and Ivan were always striving for equality, but it was always out of their reach because they did not understand what it meant to be humble, what it meant to be modest. They would never have gotten on their knees for you; your lives did not matter to them, only the masses mattered. But I understand that every one of you is important, every one of you is an individual with something to offer in this dark time.

"I beg of you, we must remain at peace with each other, and we must continue to fight for one another, not against. Roman did not have a Pure Blood upon the throne; after he lost control of Nikolai, he trusted no one. Pure Bloods, I am asking you now, are you satisfied with Tasia and Anja and their places beside me?"

There were murmurs, then an assenting voice, quickly followed by others. "Yes."

"Yes."

"Yes!"

"Yes!" The whole crowd agreed. She gave them what they wanted, and she got what she wanted in return.

Torenia waited for silence once more, before speaking again. "The Sisterhood is rising!"

"To the Sisterhood!" a voice cried.

"To the Sisterhood!" another cheered.

"To the Sisterhood!" they all joined in.

Their booming voices were a source of power, coursing through Torenia's veins, making her grin. She loomed over the gullible faces, all of them desperate for new power, a new face. Torenia was that face; they had watched her rise from nothing to become their leader. The faces that she could make out in the blur of bodies looked at her with awe. Each and every one of them longed to be her, to touch her hands, to make themselves known to her.

It was more than beauty ever was to her.

Yet she still whispered to herself. "Mirror, mirror on the wall, who's the fairest of them all?"

None of them heard her, yet they began to cheer.

"Torenia!"

"Torenia!"

"Torenia!"

EPILOGUE
THE YEAR OF THE MOON

The forests of Silvania stirred the night the curse ended, as a vibration hummed and turned into a deep echo. Trees soaked it in, swaying their branches, passing it on like pollen. A powerful curse that had resided in the town for centuries was unraveled, the blood magic that had created and bound it rippling through the earth, seeking somewhere to go. The power seeped back into the earth where it had first come from, the trees soaking it up before the air carried it along.

The wolves were the first to feel the shift when the curse that bound the once eternal Wolf to the Luca family was stripped. The whole pack began to act erratically, instinct telling them to move into the land that was once theirs. The alpha had her work cut out for her as she herded her pack back to sanity—they had much to do before they took over the forests again.

While the curse dissipated, the witches still walked.

A lowly witch with nothing but the clothes on her back and ink, quill, and parchment was the next to understand what had happened. While her skills with magic were fleeting at best, her powers of observation were keen. It was she who quietly oversaw what became of the town that had been haunted by the curse for four centuries. It was she who penned detailed accounts and had them sent to the right people, people who for centuries had a common goal they were never able to achieve, passing it down from generation to generation. For when the curse that Torenia Luca's ancestor made was severed, she became the last Luca. Her armor was dropped and her vulnerabilities began to appear.

The lowly witch sent word and word was returned.

War was coming, said simply in five words.

"Down with the Blood Queen."

ACKNOWLEDGMENTS

It's getting harder to type these without tearing up. There are a plethora of humans who have helped me reach this point. The vastness of the support is overwhelming in the best ways.

Thank you to Cassandra for taking a chance on my beloved series and giving it a home.

Thank you to Tiffany and Stephen for those tedious edits and smoothing out the rough edges.

Thank you to Kate P., the love of my life, my sweetest friend... The Juice Is Worth the Squeeze.

To the Word Weavers, for keeping me on track while also going so far off the rails.

To my family for supporting me along the way. Mum and Dad, thanks for reading, and also sorry. Some things you don't need to read, but I love you both so much.

To Cassandra, Tiff, Stephen, and everyone at Quill & Crow for believing in The Blood Bound Series.

To you, the reader, I thank you from the bottom of my heart. These books would sit on my laptop forever without you.

INDEX A

THE BLOOD BOUND SERIES TIMELINE

The Year of the Curse (1504) Azalea Luca's time/Blood Coven
The Year of the Pines (1781) Torenia is 7/Ashen Heart
The Year of Ash (1783) Song of the Sea
The Year of the Siren (1785) Song of the Sea
The Year of Gluttony (1786) Song of the Sea
The Year of the Raven (1791) Torenia is 17/Ashen Heart
The Year of the Brothers (1795) Brotherhood is won
The Year of Indulgence (1798) Torenia meets Roman/Ashen Heart
The Year of the Black Tide (1808) Song of the Sea
The Dark Years (10 years time)
The Year of the Moon (1891) Red's time/Blood Coven/Blood Queen

INDEX B
TRIGGER INDEX

This book contains the following:

Abortion (discussed)
Blood (drinking/bathing/play)
Blood Sacrifice
Child Death
Fantasy Violence
Sexual Assault (mentioned/off-screen)
Stoning to Death

ABOUT THE AUTHOR

Sabrina Voerman is a West Coaster with a penchant for visiting the numerous cemeteries across Vancouver Island. With a profound love of fairy tales and all things witchy, she draws her inspiration from the nature around her, allowing it to bleed into her storytelling. She is always seeking new adventures and places to explore, either in life or in her writing. When she isn't traversing all Vancouver Island has to offer, she can be found with a cup of coffee either reading a book or writing one.

THANK YOU FOR READING

Thank you for reading *Ashen Heart*. We deeply appreciate our readers, and are grateful for everyone who takes the time to leave us a review. If you're interested, please visit our website to find review links. Your reviews help small presses and indie authors thrive, and we appreciate your support.

Other Titles by Quill & Crow

Blood Coven

The Ancient Ones Trilogy

There Ought to be Shadows

Milton Keynes UK
Ingram Content Group UK Ltd.
UKHW040122170324
439511UK00004B/193